SIGNED

MARNI MANN

ISBN-13: 978-1983565854

For Nina Grinstead.
For being the best publicist in the entire world.
For being the most wonderful friend.
For every laugh, every yasss, every late-night call.
Signed never would have happened if it wasn't for you.
I'll never forget the lube again, I promise.
Love you.

1

JAMES

"NOTHING SAYS SINGLE LIKE BLACK VERSACE," Eve, my best friend, said from behind me as I stood in front of the mirror. "It's like the dress was made just for you."

I turned to check out the whole outfit, starting at the bottom where the fabric lay several inches above my knees, rising to hug my ass, molding across my sides, and finishing around my breasts. It was so tight; it pushed them high and gave me plenty of cleavage.

I smiled as I glanced at her reflection. "That's because it was."

"I thought your stylist dropped it off this morning?"

I shook my head. "That was Tom Ford. Versace sent this a few months ago for my eighteenth birthday."

Before choosing to wear this one, I'd tried on the Tom Ford and several others. They weren't right for tonight.

This one was.

Eve started fixing the back of my hair, and a sly grin came over her face.

"Spill it," I said.

"Abel who?" She laughs. "Seriously, once everyone sees you in this dress, they'll forget you two even dated."

The trouble was, I hadn't forgotten.

I'd met Abel on the set of my first sitcom when I was only thirteen. We were the same age, casted to be siblings, and we'd kept those roles until the series finale five years later. Our relationship had started almost immediately and ended six months ago when I caught him in our bed with Sophia Sully.

I turned toward her. "He's on location, right?"

We shared friends. Favorite bars. A house that I no longer wanted.

I would die if he and Sophia were there tonight since the only reason I was going out was to make it look like I was completely over him and had moved on.

"Let me check." Eve slipped her phone out of the top of her dress and opened a social media app. She held her cell in front of me, and the screen showed a picture that had been taken a few hours ago of Abel riding a fake bull. "He's at some bar in Nashville. We're safe."

I took a few steps closer to the glass, so I could get a better look at myself. There was loose powder under my eyes that my makeup artist had missed. I caught it with my fingers and then smoothed out the chunks of curls to frame them around my face.

I'd been filming in Toronto for the last four months, and this was my first night back. While I'd been away, Abel and Sophia had made their relationship public. He'd moved her into the house we'd purchased together. They'd bought a puppy and named it Country, as though they needed to be reminded of the kind of music Sophia sang.

Because the LA crowd had barely seen me since the breakup, I was going to be hit with questions, and the paparazzi would be snapping my picture as soon as I got to the bar. So, I had to get it all right—the answers everyone wanted to hear, the dress, and most importantly, the smile. The same smile that the whole world loved. The one that earned me leading roles. The one that acted like a mask, so no one could tell I was hurting.

I could do this.

"Fuck Abel," I whispered.

"Yeah, fuck Abel," she repeated. She grabbed my clutch off the bathroom counter and looped her arm through mine. "Now, let's go find you a rebound."

"I tried that once, don't you remember? I'm all set."

Since ending things with Abel, I'd been with only one guy, and it was three months ago. I'd flown home from filming in Toronto to move out of the house I shared with Abel. Sophia had watched me the whole time I was there and again at the party I'd seen them at later that night. The guy was someone I had just met, and he was supposed to make me feel like I had moved on. I had gone with him to a hotel in Malibu, and after the next morning, we never spoke again.

"Then, let's go get wasted," Eve said.

"I can do that."

She pulled me through the house and out the door, knowing I'd never feel fully ready to face this and dragging me was probably the only way she'd get me there. Once we got outside, the SUV was waiting in my driveway.

"Where to, Miss Ryne?" the driver asked as we settled and put on our seat belts.

"Chateau Marmont," I told him.

As we made our way to West Hollywood, Eve filled me in on the gossip I'd missed while I was away, things that hadn't made the celebrity news sites. None of the people she spoke about were good friends even though most of their numbers were saved in my phone. Not one of them had checked on me after the breakup, although they'd texted me tonight to ask if I was going out.

They wanted to be seen with me.

That was the way Hollywood worked, and I'd been playing this game since I was a kid. Except, when I had been with Abel, there wasn't this pressure to go out and be seen in order to stay relevant. The public had loved our relationship, and that was enough to keep the paparazzi on our asses. But, without him, the media wanted to see what the single version of me looked like.

I was about to give them that visual.

The driver pulled up in front, and the backseat door was immediately opened. A hand was extended to help me out, and I waited for Eve, looping her arm through mine as she reached me.

We walked toward the entrance, and hundreds of cameras flashed in our direction.

Questions were being thrown at me.

"How are you feeling after the breakup?"

"What's the next movie you'll be starring in?"

And, "Should your fans stop listening to country music?"

The smile was glued across my lips as I glanced at both sides of the crowd, giving them a final wave before we disappeared inside the dark bar. The darkness was one of the reasons I enjoyed coming here. The red and gold back lighting didn't just make it dim and sexy, but it also hid runny makeup and accidental nip slips—something certainly possible with a dress cut this low. And, as if those rich colors didn't already set the most seductive vibe, the heavy wood furnishings and the smell of leather brought it right over the top.

"Drink," I said to Eve as I took in the room.

She brought me straight to the bar where the bartender greeted us with, "Good to have you back, James."

If you were anyone in this town, you were called by your first name and you were never asked for an ID. I always tried my hardest to remember my favorites. Tony was one.

The smile still hadn't left my face. "Two cosmos, Tony. Charge them to my account, please."

"You got it," he answered.

"Everyone is here," Eve said, facing the opposite direction as me, so she could wave at the people passing.

There was a mirror behind the bar, and that was what I used to scan the room. I saw a group of regulars standing in the middle, who we'd chat with once we had our drinks. A few Hollywood old-timers were sitting on barstools around the high-tops. With the amount of celebrities here, this place was practically an audition, and I was sure they were scouting. Leaning around the front of the bar was a musician, a few LA hockey players, and *him*—a man who was four people over, whose eyes locked with mine.

Eyes that made my lips part.

Eyes that made my chest feel tight and anxious.

He was deliciously handsome—from his messy, gelled hair to his square jaw and the dark scruff that covered it.

I didn't know his name.

I had no idea who he was.

But he had to be someone if he'd gotten in here.

Asking would give me a reason to look away, to take a break from those eyes that were holding me captive.

Since my attraction to him was already so obvious by the way I was staring, I turned toward Eve and whispered, "Who is he?"

She glanced in both directions. "Who's who?"

"The hottie at the bar four people down from me. All dark everything—suit, tie. You'll know him when you see him."

A few seconds passed, and she said, "I have no idea whom you're talking about."

"Oh my God," I sighed, glancing back at the mirror. "He's the one—" I cut myself off when I realized he was no longer standing there. I looked across the bar, over the group in the middle, and on the side near the restrooms.

He was gone.

"Two cosmos," Tony said, setting them in front of us. "Can I get you girls anything else?"

"No, thank you," I said, grabbing my drink and holding it up in front of me. "Let's toast." I quickly gazed over my shoulder to see if the guy had come back. He hadn't. "To tonight, being single, being back together after two months apart, and being best bitches."

"To not remembering anything in the morning." She hit her glass against mine. "Oh, and to Abel, fuck you."

I laughed, and we each took our first sip.

Cosmo number one went down so quickly, and so did the second. After round three, I completely lost track, and I was sure our toasts had started to repeat. I knew it was time to switch to water when I was coming out of the restroom, and my heel got caught in the carpet. As I tried to take a step, my foot came out of my shoe, and I tripped.

Someone's hands gripped my waist from behind and caught me before I hit the ground.

"Thank you," I panted, using their fingers to steady myself.

Once I was sure everything was in place—the bottom of my dress was down, and the top was covering my breasts—I turned to see whom the hands belonged to.

My breath hitched when I saw his face. "It's you," I said.

I knew that made no sense to him, but it made perfect sense to me.

It was the guy who had been standing at the bar.

Whose eyes had held me hostage.

Who had made me feel anxious.

Who was making my chest tight again.

He laughed, and the movement showed me a smile that caused a tingle between my legs. A grin that would make him the most famous person in here if the world saw him on the big screen. That was how I knew he was either just starting out or wasn't in the field at all.

"Most people call me Brett."

Even though I'd slipped my heel back on, he was still about four inches taller than me and looked even sexier now that I was so close to him. The lines in his forehead and the crinkles just to the sides of his eyes told me he was in his late twenties or early thirties—certainly a lot older than me. All that meant was, he had experience, and that was the biggest turn-on.

"I'm James."

He said nothing and made no attempt to move.

"I saw you at the bar, and then you were gone."

"And?"

That voice.

If sex had a sound, it was Brett's tone.

"Is someone expecting you to return, or am I about to get jumped by some jealous girlfriend or..."

"Or what?"

I started to speak and stumbled over my words.

How can I tell this man with the beautiful eyes that I don't want him to walk away because I can't get enough of the way he looks at me and the warmth I feel from his stare?

"Or maybe I could hear more of your voice," I said.

He licked across the inside of his bottom lip, and when he exhaled, I tasted the whiskey on his breath and smelled the cologne from his skin. It was a mix of spice and sandalwood, and it made every pore in my body open up and want to suck him in.

"All you want is my voice?"

I broke our contact again, almost dizzy from the intensity, and took a step back to lean against the wall behind me. Brett followed. His arm went up in the air, his hand pressing on the space above my head. He didn't touch me. He didn't have to. Having him huddled over me, caging me in, did so much to my body that I couldn't breathe.

2

BRETT

AS JAMES THOUGHT about my question, her hungry eyes
stared into mine. She wanted more than my voice; I could tell
that by the way she looked at me. Fuck, I could tell that from
when she had been gawking at me at the bar. I hadn't been able to
walk over and give her attention out there.

I could now.

"Answer me," I demanded.

She blinked, her lashes so long that the movement was
delayed.

My free hand wrapped around her neck, and I used my
thumb to hold her chin up. Soft, perfect skin, not a single flaw
anywhere on her face.

That was because she was only eighteen.

Eighteen.

And that was twelve goddamn years younger than me.

*Jesus, what the hell am I doing? If the guys and Scarlett were
here, they'd give me so much shit.*

James's mouth opened, her natural, pouty lips fucking
tempting me. The tip of her tongue swept across her bottom

teeth, and I could picture her doing the same to my cock, circling the crown and then surrounding it to suck.

Maybe her age—for tonight—was something I could overlook.

I held her tighter as I rubbed my nose over her cheek. Her skin smelled of pears, her hair like raspberries. "This will help you decide."

My lips touched hers, and she let out the softest groan.

She leaned forward, pressing her body onto mine, a hand now snaking up my stomach and moving toward my chest. When she got to the back of my head, I pulled away.

Her eyes were slow to open, but as they did, the hunger turned feral.

All we'd shared was a kiss.

I hadn't touched her body, hadn't put my mouth below her neck.

I hadn't even called her by her name.

I wanted more than my lips on hers. I wanted her naked. I wanted my tongue on her body and her nails stabbing my back.

I wanted to hear her moan my name.

"Come home with me," I said.

My hand dropped from the wall, and I cupped her other cheek, looking from one eye to the other, trying to see her thoughts. There was a war going on in there, and I wanted to ease it. So, I pressed my lips behind her ear and kissed all the way around it until I reached her cheek.

"Mmm," she breathed.

"I just want to taste you."

"Brett..."

Fuck, I love the sound of that.

"What do you want, James?"

"I want to leave with you."

I had to be sure, so I growled, "Say it again."

She tried to stand taller to kiss me, and I let her get one in but stopped her after a few seconds.

"Again, James, or the only place I'm taking you is to find your friend."

"I want to go home with you. Right now."

I was holding her with so much force, I knew I could be hurting her, but my need to have her was greater than the control I was trying to exhibit.

"I have a car waiting out back," I said.

Before catching her, I had been on my way out to hit up another spot, meeting with clients at both bars. But, as I'd been walking past her toward the door, she'd tripped, and I'd grabbed her before she could fall. Now, I didn't want to take another step unless my hands were somewhere on her.

"What are we waiting for then?"

I'd tasted booze on her lips, and I wanted to make sure she could move on her own, that she didn't have more than a strong buzz, or I wouldn't be taking her anywhere. So, I took a step back toward the door, giving her enough space that she'd have to walk.

"You good?"

She followed without so much as a wobble and said, "Let me just text Eve and let her know."

She pulled out her phone, and I watched her fingers hit the screen. Then, she slid her cell back into the bag and shut it. "Ready."

I connected our bodies, holding her waist again, thinking of the distance between here and my car. "Do you want me to carry you?"

"If that means we'll get there faster, then yes."

I wrapped an arm under her knees and another around her back, and I picked her up. I held her against my chest as I brought her through the door and into the alley behind the bar.

The SUV was close to the exit, the engine already running.

The driver opened the backseat door, and I placed James inside and said, "Home," to him before I climbed in.

"I never knew you could go out that way," she said as she settled in her seat. "Man, do you know how many ugly shots that could have saved me? The paps park right outside the front, and the photos they take late at night can be so unflattering. You have no idea what it's like when the world sees you at your worst."

I was in the industry; I understood how it worked.

She obviously didn't know that.

"Do you live far from here?" she asked.

Her body was leaning into mine, shivering from the air-conditioning vent blowing right above her. I pointed the air in the opposite direction, and my other hand went into her hair, pulling her face toward mine.

"A couple of miles," I hissed against her lips, parting them for me.

The cranberry juice she'd mixed with her vodka tasted so fucking sweet on her tongue. If she gave me any more of it, I was going to shred her dress right here, dip my face between her legs, and lick her cunt.

Fuck, I couldn't wait to taste that pussy and see if it was as sweet as the juice.

This driver needed to step on it.

I wasn't a patient man.

As if she sensed that, she pulled back just a little, and I bit into her bottom lip, holding it, tugging it, before I said, "I'm going to fucking devour you." Finally releasing her, I turned my attention to her neck, smelling, kissing, gnawing the skin that led to her ear.

"Oh my God," she groaned, and she tried to slide her fingers through the slots between the buttons of my shirt.

She went lower, brushing back and forth across my cock, and that was when I shackled her wrists in my hand.

"Please," she whined.

"You're going to get it all fucking night; don't you worry."

We pulled into the front of my high-rise and came to a stop, and I opened the back door.

"I've got it, sir," the driver said.

"I'm good," I replied, sliding James into my arms and carrying her out.

The doorman didn't greet me by name, a sign that he was new, but held the door open for us, and I took us through the lobby and into the elevator.

James's tongue traced the outline of my ear as I pressed the button for my floor and settled us against the back wall.

"Make it hurry," she breathed.

My thoughts were the same.

When we got to my floor, I rushed us down the short hallway and waved my fob over the reader. It clicked as it unlocked, and I brought us into the bedroom, setting James on her feet right by the bed.

I stood in front of her and said, "Turn around."

I waited until her back faced me, and then I kissed across it while I lowered the zipper at the same time. She turned again when I was done, and she let the dress fall to the floor.

The only thing she wore now was the pair of black heels.

No bra, no panties.

I leaned back to admire her body. She had tits that were no bigger than my palms, nipples that were small and hard, and a bare pussy with the sweetest fucking clit at the top.

"Jesus Christ," I moaned. She went to take the heels off, and I said, "Hell no. Keep them on."

I looped my finger into the Windsor knot and pulled it loose. Before I had it off, James fisted both ends of my tie and used them to pull me toward her. The movement caused my lips to slam against hers, and the tie slithered down my chest, followed by the buttons from my shirt that she had torn apart.

She wanted my cock.

She was getting my tongue first.

I slipped my arms out of the shirt, dropped the pants, socks, and shoes, and then I guided her onto the bed. Her head hit the middle of the mattress, and I bent her knees, spreading them wide, my face diving between them.

"*Ahhh!*" she screamed as I licked her clit.

Her cunt tasted even sexier than her mouth.

Usually, I'd take my time with it. Lapping it, teasing her, until she begged, until she dug her nails into my scalp and screamed for more pressure.

Not tonight.

Tonight was about learning her pussy, swallowing all of her wetness, and leaving some of my own. I memorized this view, so this would be the image I saw when I got on the plane tomorrow morning and closed my eyes to sleep through the long flight.

I inserted a finger and then a second one, licking with the same speed as I was finger-fucking her.

"Brett," she groaned. "You're going to make me come."

I clenched her ass and lifted her higher on the bed, giving me enough room to reach the nightstand where I grabbed a condom and ripped it open with my teeth.

"My God," she said as I pulled down my boxer briefs, my cock springing free now that nothing was holding it back. Her eyes widened as she watched me roll the rubber over it.

I knew better than to slam right into her.

I wouldn't break her.

She'd learn that soon enough.

"Your body..." Her eyes finally left my dick and rose past my abs to my chest and back down. "It's insane."

Kneeling in front of her, I put her legs over my shoulders,

gripped her ass, and aimed my cock at her entrance. She was so wet, my crown slipped right in.

"Fuck," I hissed as I pushed in another inch. "You're so fucking tight."

My fingers moved to her clit, rubbing it as I went in a little deeper. Her moans told me she could handle it. So, still going slow, I sank in further. When I was almost all the way in, I stopped to let her spread around me.

She was so fucking turned on, her pussy was pulsing, her clit hardening the more I circled it.

I waited several seconds, and then I reared back and gently thrust in. As she got used to my size, I felt her start to relax, and I went in a little harder.

"More!" she yelled.

And I knew she was close.

I wanted her to come but not here.

I wrapped her legs around my waist and carried her to the closest wall. Using it to hold her weight, I now had full access to her pussy, and it was dripping all over my balls. The short hairs above my cock were positioned against her clit, giving her the same kind of friction as my finger. When she felt it, she groaned.

My speed increased, letting the power in my legs take control.

I was going deeper, harder, my balls tightening more with each pump.

"Yesss," she cried out.

And I felt her clench around my dick.

I twisted my hips as I plunged in and growled, "Come."

She shuddered immediately, her pussy constricting around me, her moan so loud that it vibrated through my body.

I didn't stop.

I drove straight through her orgasm, and when I felt her calm,

I moved us over to the bed. I sat with my back against the headboard and barked, "Ride me until I come."

She pressed her hands on my chest and worked her body up and down. I loved watching the lips of her cunt spread as it swallowed my cock, the way her tits bounced with each stroke, how her flat stomach flexed, how her head fell back as I reached a spot that felt so good.

"Faster," I commanded.

She kept me inside but rocked her hips back and forth.

I put a thumb on her clit, flicking it, and another on her nipple. "That's it, James."

Her pussy began to contract around me.

"You're going to come again; I can feel it."

A tingling sensation spread through my balls. "Shit," I roared, "you're so tight, you're sucking the cum out of me." I leaned forward to take her nipple into my mouth, biting around it as my first load shot into the condom.

"Oh God," she cried, her stomach quivering, telling me she was at the peak.

I gripped her ass and tilted my hips, giving her a few more thrusts until the only movement was our breathing.

Gently, I pulled her off me and set her on the bed, dipping my face down to her thighs. As I tried to separate them, she fought me.

That was when I looked up and said, "It'll feel good if I lick it, especially if you're sore."

She released the tension in her muscles, and I positioned my lips over her cunt, swiping up to her clit and down until I got close to her ass.

"*Breeett*," she moaned, gripping my hair, yanking it between her fingers. "You're going to make me come again."

I knew that would be the result, but putting my mouth here was more for me than her. I hadn't gotten enough of it earlier, and because I didn't know if I'd ever get to taste it again, I wanted to stay right here until my tongue felt raw.

———

Several hours later, I slipped out of bed and took a shower, putting on a fresh suit once I dried. Since I kept a wardrobe here, I didn't need to travel with a suitcase. The housekeeper made sure my place was clean, and she laundered all my clothes.

Finishing up in the bathroom, I squirted gel into my hair and worked it through the strands. Then, I sprayed some cologne on my neck. When I came out, James was still in the same position, lying on her stomach near the middle of the bed. The blanket only covered the lower part of her back, showing the outline of that perfect fucking ass.

Damn it, I wish I had time to taste her again.

I walked over and gave her a kiss on the forehead.

She stirred, her eyes slowly opening, and she rolled onto her back. As soon as the air hit her nipples, they turned hard. "Where are you going?" she asked.

"Home."

She rubbed the corners of her eyes, looking briefly around the bedroom. "Home? You mean, this isn't your place?"

"It is."

She pulled the blanket up to her neck. "Where's home then?"

"Miami."

I took the piece of paper out of my pocket that I'd written on when I got out of the shower and set it next to her on the bed. "That's my number." I moved toward the bedroom door and said, "When you're ready to go, hit nine on the phone on the night-stand, and that'll call the doorman. All you have to do is give him your name. By the time you get downstairs, my driver will be waiting for you."

She sat up, holding the blanket against her.

She was even gorgeous the morning after.

"When will I see you again?"

I narrowed my lids, taking in the last of her face, memorizing the way she stared at me, the way her body looked in my bed. "When I'm back in LA," I said, and I shut the door behind me.

3

JAMES

Me: You're not going to believe what happened last night.
Eve: Where are you?
Me: Getting a ride home.
Eve: From where?
Me: Some building near The Beverly Hilton, I think.
Eve: Start talking.
Me: I had the most insane sex. INSANE.
Eve: With whom?
Me: A guy from the bar. His name's Brett.
Eve: I know a million of those.
Me: Not like this one, I promise.
Eve: What's his last name?
Me: I don't know.
Eve: Remember when you said you weren't interested in another rebound? I'm glad you didn't listen to yourself.
Me: I remember you telling me, when Abel and I broke up, that the best way to get over a guy was to get under another one.
Consider this round two.

Eve: I'm LOLing so hard right now. God, I give the best advice.
When do I get to meet him?
Me: Eh, he doesn't live here.
Eve: He lives...
Me: Miami.
Eve: Jesus.
Me: But it was insane. Insane. Insane. Insane.
Eve: Then, who the fuck cares where he lives?
Me: Exactly.
Eve: I need details. Brunch?
Me: I'll meet you on Melrose in an hour.
Eve: That's my bitch.

4

BRETT

I HELD on to the railing and rushed up the short staircase, ducking my head so that I wouldn't bump it when I stepped inside the private plane.

"Mr. Young," the flight attendant said as I straightened, "it's nice to have you back."

"Morning." I took a seat mid-plane, opening my computer and setting it on the table in front of me.

She stood in the aisle next to me. "Can I get you your usual to drink?"

"Please," I replied, taking a grape off the fruit tray and popping it into my mouth as I watched my email load.

There was so much fucking work waiting for me back in Miami. I knew my team was on top of it. I knew they were as productive there as I had been in LA. But I also knew that, after tonight, I would be putting in some long hours at the office.

Scanning the subject line of each email, I read what was important and trashed all the bullshit. When I made it through about a quarter of the list, I opened a new email, addressed it to my support staff, and typed.

. . .

I MET WITH SMITH LAST NIGHT AT THE CHATEAU
MARMONT. HE'S READY TO SIGN. HAVE LEGAL PREPARE THE
CONTRACT, USING THE NUMBERS WE DISCUSSED YESTERDAY,
AND RUN IT THROUGH SCARLETT'S DEPARTMENT, SO THEY
CAN GET IT INTO THE BILLING SYSTEM.

BMW IS SHOPPING FOR A NEW FACE FOR THEIR PRINT
AND COMMERCIAL AD CAMPAIGNS. SMITH WILL BE PERFECT
FOR THEM. PUT TOGETHER A PITCH AND INCLUDE HIS PRESS
MATERIALS. IT'S A $15-MILLION-DOLLAR CONTRACT, AND I
WANT IT AWARDED TO THE AGENCY, SO HAVE IT DONE BY THE
TIME I RETURN.

JACK THINKS HE'S GOT THIS MONTH IN THE BAG. LET'S
MAKE SURE HE DOESN'T.

"Here you go," the flight attendant said as she set a Bloody Mary
on the table. "Can I get you anything else?"

I shook my head and pulled out my phone. Since the office
and half of my clients were on East Coast time, I had almost a
hundred texts that had come through in the last thirty minutes.

There wasn't one from James.

I hadn't asked for her number. All it would take was a
phone call to my office, and someone on my staff would get it
for me.

I wouldn't do that.

I'd overlooked her age for one night. That night was over, and
I was a man of my word.

If we talked again, it would be on her.

The pilot called the phone that was next to my seat and said,
"We're scheduled to take off in four minutes, so we're going to
start taxiing toward the runway. We expect a few bumps as we

pass over the southeast corner of New Mexico, but overall, it should be a fairly smooth ride."

I thanked him and hung up. Pressing a button that lifted the leg rest, I reclined the top of my seat. Using the remote that was on the table, I flipped through the satellite stations until I found the news.

I swallowed the Bloody Mary in a few gulps and relaxed into my seat.

James's face was the first thing I saw when I closed my eyes.

James Ryne.

America's sweetheart.

And one hell of a fuck.

Someone who, after last night, had proven to be more sexually mature than a lot of the women I'd slept with. She never told me not to fuck her so hard, never begged me to slow down. And she'd rocked those hips just the way I liked to be ridden.

Eighteen was certainly the youngest I'd ever been with.

Jesus, I'd stooped pretty low this time.

But her pussy had felt so good and had tasted even better.

I finished the last of my scotch and set the tumbler on our table inside the VIP room of the bar. It wasn't there for more than a few seconds before our waitress came over, grabbed the bottle from the center of our table, and refilled my glass. She then moved on to Jack's glass and finally to Max's.

"Can I get you gentlemen anything?" She adjusted the collar of her shirt, the V now showing the black lace of her bra. Last week, it had been pink.

I reached into my pocket, searching for the hundred I'd put in there earlier, and handed it to her. "Come back in twenty."

She smiled as she pulled the bill out of my fingers, and I

turned my attention to Jack as he said, "Look at that goddamn number." He was holding his cell in the air, pointing at the bottom of an email. "Twelve million this month."

I'd already seen the email on the plane this morning, so I knew Jack, who headed up the sports division of our company, had been listed as the top earner so far this month. As soon as Smith was signed to the acting division that I managed and BMW was locked in, my number would double his. Coming in last place was the music sector, which Max was in charge of, at four million.

All three departments made up The Agency, a company I'd opened five years ago with my three best friends, and it was now the largest entertainment agency in Florida.

"Jesus Christ," I groaned. "I'm not listening to this shit again. We know how well you're doing. Give it a fucking rest."

"Why, Brett?" Jack asked. "Having a hard time with second place?" He leaned into the leather couch and crossed his arms behind his head. "When are you pussies going to bring me a real game? You're making this shit too easy on me."

"Ten thousand says I'm number one next month," Max said.

"I'll take that bet," I said, loosening my tie.

The R&B singer Max would be signing next week was one of the top in the world. Her contract would be impressive but still not as large as Smith's. And, when I added Smith and BMW to my forecast along with the renewal of the TV judge, Oscar winner, reality star, and the other deals the agents on my team were negotiating, it would be one of the acting departments largest months.

"Fuck that," Jack said to Max. "I want your Vanquish, and then we'll have a deal."

The Aston Martin Vanquish was Max's baby, and it was one sexy fucking baby. The car had more horsepower than all three of Jack's cars combined.

"My department has no problem with keeping up. It's your team that doesn't fill out the paperwork correctly."

The screen of my phone lit up with a text.

James: I'm a little sore...and I could use some healing.
Me: If I were in LA, my tongue would be all yours.

"Brett, I saw Smith's contract before I left the office," Scarlett whispered. Her quiet tone was because I'd texted her from the plane and told her to keep it a secret from the guys. "You had some tough competition. LA was determined not to lose him. New York has been scouting him for months. I'm damn proud of you."

I smiled at her. "That one negotiated hard."

"But you got what you wanted, and so did he."

"Hey," Max yelled. "What are you two whispering about?"

Scarlett turned toward him and said, "Brett was just telling me about the new curtains he's buying for his living room."

"What the hell?" Max snapped. "You're such a fucking liar."

I squeezed her shoulder as I laughed.

James: Get on a plane.
Me: I just got off one.

As I gazed up from my phone, I saw the owner of the bar walking over to us.

He stopped in between my couch and Jack's and said, "Brett, Scarlett, Jack, Max, thanks for joining us tonight."

"Always a pleasure," Scarlett replied.

"How's everything this evening?" he asked. "I hope your cocktail waitress, Natalie, is treating you all right?"

"No complaints," I said.

"She's doing a fine job," Max said.

"Good to hear," he said. "You know we're happy to reserve a table for you any night of the week, so if there's anything I can do, anything you need at all, don't hesitate to reach out. You all have my personal cell number."

I shook his hand, and then my eyes went to my phone.

James: Will this help persuade you?

A picture of James loaded onto my screen.
Fuck me.

It only showed her from the waist down, the small freckle on the inside of her thigh proving it was her. She had on the sexiest pair of lace panties, and her hand was reaching into the front of them.

She was touching herself.

Me: It doesn't hurt.

"Texting anyone important?" Jack asked.

When I looked up, the three of them were staring at me. I turned my phone around, so the screen faced my lap and said, "Nah, just a client."

"Now, he's the one lying," Max snapped.

"Scarlett, take his phone, and check out who he's been texting," Jack said.

"We all know Brett would never hand over his phone," she said. "And, even though I think I'm a badass at the gym, there's no way I'm strong enough to pry it from his fingers." She smiled as she gazed at me. "Just fess up. Did you meet someone in LA?"

My eyes scanned all three of their faces. "Maybe."

"I fucking knew it," Jack said. "Who is she?"

"She's nothing yet," I replied.

"Not what I asked," he came back with.

"I know what you fucking asked, Jack, and right now, that's all you're getting."

"You're so stubborn," Scarlett said.

There were lots of comebacks I could make, but Scarlett didn't deserve that. She was speaking the truth; I was fucking stubborn.

That didn't mean I was going to say a word about James. As far as I was concerned, that conversation was locked.

James: When can I see you?

I scrolled through my Calendar app and went back to the text conversation.

Me: Couple of weeks maybe.
James: I hate waiting.
Me: We have that in common.
James: Tell me something good.
Me: I'm going to look at your photo while I stroke my cock tonight.
James: I wish I could see that.

"Looks like you're running a little low," the waitress said, holding the empty bottle in her hand after only refilling Jack's glass.

"We'll have another bottle," I told her.

"Shit," Max groaned. "It's going to be a long night."

5

JAMES

"JAMES, turn your face a little to the left," the photographer said.

Even though the position was extremely uncomfortable, I shifted my neck in the direction he'd asked and tried to keep the rest of my body still.

"Good," he said. "Now, make your smile bigger." He paused while I adjusted. "Just like that." A few more clicks of the camera and then, "Look down just a smidge." He shifted to the right and then straight in front of me. "*Yesss.* Don't move."

I wasn't moving.

I wasn't breathing.

I was just sweating under these super-bright set lights and sticking to the white table they had my arms propped against, hoping the towel wrapped around me wouldn't fall. Even though the set stylist had told me she clamped the pins extra tight, I could feel them loosening.

"Bigger, bigger," the photographer complained. "Show me passion; show me emotion."

Whenever I did a shoot for Dior, I always worked with this

photographer, so I knew what he expected from me. This time, it was to show their new line of eye shadow. The picture chosen from today's shoot would run in an international campaign with billboards, product displays at all department stores that carried the brand, and online ads, and there would be a digital screen displayed in Times Square.

And my face was melting off.

I couldn't imagine how much retouching these shots would need.

"Turn, turn—no, the other way. Yes, turn that way. Turn, turn, turn. Now, stop." He continued to look through his lens, but I didn't hear the clicking of the camera. "Uh, makeup?" he called. "Where's makeup? James is looking shiny."

"I'm here," the makeup artist said, running over to blot my cheeks and powder the spots that needed blending.

When she finished, the photographer looked through his camera again and said, "Let's take twenty." He pointed at the makeup artist. "Clean her up. Start over if you have to. The powder caked to clammy skin isn't a pretty look, sweetheart." He looked at the group of set assistants. "One of you, get James a fan."

I reached around to my back and grabbed the towel, so it wouldn't fly open when I stood.

The makeup artist went behind me and said, "Here, let me help." She readjusted each pin to make it tighter and then handed me a robe.

"Thank you," I said, tying it around my waist.

"Let's head back to the dressing room, so I can touch up the rest of your makeup."

I followed her into one of the back rooms, the same place I'd left my clothes and purse, and I grabbed my phone before taking a seat on the high stool. While she slathered more concealer over my forehead, I scrolled through my texts.

There was one from Eve, asking how the shoot was. I typed back that it was going okay and I would see her later when we met for dinner. Then, I opened the message from Brett, which was a reply to the question that I had asked him earlier—*Are you going to tell me what you do?*

> *Brett: I'm an attorney.*
> *Me: What kind?*
> *Brett: One who always wins.*

The thought made me smile, as it didn't surprise me one bit.

He had so much power in his body, I was sure he brought even more to the courtroom.

I could picture him in a custom-tailored suit, like the one he'd worn to Chateau Marmont, walking up to the stand to completely demolish a witness's testimony.

> *Me: Maybe I need to hire you.*
> *Brett: For what?*
> *Me: For something in LA that requires your immediate presence.*
> *Brett: Immediate isn't possible, but I can help in the interim.*
> *Me: How?*
> *Brett: Take that thumb you're using to type and run it down your body until it hits your clit, and then...*

I went to the Home screen and pressed the icon for the camera, holding the phone up and to the side to take a selfie.

I attached it to my text and typed.

> *Me: I'm at a photo shoot.*
> *Brett: Fuck, you're gorgeous.*
> *Me: Fuck, I want to hear your voice.*

In the month we'd been talking, he hadn't sent me a picture of himself, but we'd video-chatted a bunch of times. One of the things I loved about that was getting to see his eyes. It had been too dark in the bar that night to notice their color, and I'd been too preoccupied at his condo to really take a good look. But, now, I knew everything about them. His irises were a piercing sea green that darkened to emerald near the pupil, and there were tiny specks of gold that weaved through the middle and stretched to the outer edge.

I was obsessed with them.

He knew that.

But he also knew I loved his voice, and I always wanted more of it.

The text screen changed to an incoming call, and Brett's name appeared.

"Hello?"

"Is this what you wanted?"

My face started to blush. It was his tone, the deepness of his words. The way they ended in just a tiny growl, reminding me of the louder ones he'd made that night at his place.

"Yes," I answered.

"What are you shooting?"

"Dior makeup."

"What's underneath the towel?"

The makeup artist turned on a portable fan and pointed it at me, and then she returned to powdering my cheeks.

"A little more than what was underneath my dress."

"Fuck," he hissed. "I need you to show it to me."

"Tonight," I promised. "Hey, you told me your assistant would be working on your travel schedule today, so what week are you coming?"

"Do you want me to surprise you?"

The anxiousness in my chest made it hard to sit still. "What

does that mean? You'll show up at my door? At my next shoot?
That you're outside right now?"

He laughed, and that was another sound that drove me mad.
So deep and honest and manly.

"It means, something you won't expect."

"Now, I'm kinda nervous."

"I'm not coming to scare you, James. I'm coming to give your
body more pleasure than you've ever felt."

I turned down the volume on my phone to make sure the
makeup artist couldn't hear what he was saying. "You mean, it
can get better than that night?"

"Yes."

That was hard to believe.

Since Abel had been my first, I'd learned everything from
him, and we'd had great sex. He'd pushed me to try things that I
hadn't thought I'd like but ended up loving.

Like anal.

I was sure Brett was well experienced with that. Still, I wasn't
sure I could handle a dick as large as his without a ridiculous
amount of prepping.

The thought made me squirm a little.

When I had been with the Malibu hotel guy, I'd tried to relax
and enjoy the feel of his foreign hands. But, after being with Abel
for so long, most of it had just felt wrong. I couldn't get Abel out
of my head, and half of the time, I had pretended it was him and
not Malibu.

And then there was the night I'd had with Brett, and that was
completely different than anything I'd had before.

It was hotter.

More intense.

It'd consumed me to where I no longer had control over my
body.

And, now, he was saying he could give me more than what he already had.

"Wow," was all I could say.

One of the photographer's assistants poked her head into the room and said, "We need you back on the set in two."

The makeup artist pulled her brush off my eyelid and put it back in the holder she wore at her waist. "I'll see you out there," she said.

I watched her leave and got up from the stool, moving over to my purse.

"You have to go," Brett said.

"I do," I said. "Can I call you when I get out?"

"I'll call you."

He said good-bye and hung up, and I slipped the phone back in my bag and returned to the set.

Since the break, someone had removed the table, and now, there was a white rug on the floor and a green screen behind it.

"You'll be standing for this part," the photographer said.

I handed the robe to the makeup artist, and she checked the pins behind me to make sure the towel was secure. When I felt it tighten, I dropped my arms to my sides.

"Now, look over here"—the photographer snapped his left hand above his head—"and give me that million-dollar smile."

It was more like three million, which was a half-million-dollar raise from the last Dior shoot.

"More left, more left. Yes, like that. Now, look at me from over your shoulder," he ordered.

I took a step back to position my body, and as I pointed my chin across my shoulder, I heard a beep. That was followed by a chime and a siren, even a bark—all sounds coming from the phones in this room. It became even louder as more cells received whatever messages were coming through.

Everyone looked around, and I could tell they were questioning whether they should take out their phones.

The photographer was the first person to dip into his pocket, and then they all followed.

The room turned silent.

I stood in a towel, the only one in here who wasn't holding a phone, hoping someone would glance up so that they could tell me what was going on.

Finally, I caught eyes with the makeup artist, and I mouthed, *What's happening?*

She seemed nervous, hesitant, and extremely uncomfortable as her stare moved to the photographer's assistant, who wore the same expression on his face. Then, slowly, the makeup artist walked over to me, holding the phone out so that I could see the screen.

A celebrity alert had come through, the message in a bright red box with white lettering.

It had my name on it.

It had other words that I couldn't comprehend.

Words that couldn't even be possible.

"We're shutting down the set!" one of Dior's representatives yelled across the room. I could tell she didn't want to turn in my direction but finally did and said, "We'll reach out to your team if we decide to reschedule." She quickly glared at the photographer. "You're off the clock," she said to him. Then, she pointed at the lighting crew. "Turn off the lights, and get the set cleared before we're billed for another hour."

Not a single person in here would look at me.

I heard the sound of their feet moving across the concrete floor and the snap that the lights made when they were shut off.

Is this really happening?

I needed answers.

I needed the alert retracted and an apology that was a mile long.

I needed to sue whoever had aired this because they certainly didn't have their facts straight, and they'd confused what they saw or heard or had in their possession.

I wouldn't do what they were accusing me of.

Not ever.

I couldn't stand here for another second.

I squeezed the front of the towel, so it wouldn't fall and rushed into the hallway and into the dressing room where I threw on my clothes and shoes. Holding my bag over my shoulder, I bolted out the door and found my car in the parking lot, shoving myself inside and scrambling to find my phone.

There were so many texts, so many social media tags, so many alerts now coming through from every site, even the news channels, that my phone was slow to load. When I finally got to the Home screen, I went to my call log and hit the number for Tim, the manager who had been with me since the start of my career.

"James," he said as he answered. "I just got in my car, and I'm driving to you right now. You're still at the photo shoot?"

The photographer walked out the same door I'd come through, and he scanned the lot until our eyes met. During the shoot, he had looked at me like I was a piece of art. Now, he wore a dirty, smoldering smirk.

I glanced away, a wave of nausea passing through me. "Tim, what the fuck is going on?"

"I don't know. I found out the same time you did."

"This can't be right. It's impossible. I didn't do it. Do you hear me? I didn't do it. Make them take it back. Make them retract that alert from every person's phone before my entire life is ruined."

Several seconds of silence passed before he said, "I'll do everything I can."

6

BRETT

I CHECKED the itinerary my assistant had emailed me and forwarded it to my team, so they knew my schedule for the next several days. I'd be arriving in LA tomorrow around noon, spending the first few hours in meetings, and then the chef I'd hired would cook dinner for James and me at my place. The next two days would look the same. Depending on James's availability, I would either fly back the morning of the fourth day or the fifth.

She had no idea when I was coming.

I liked it that way.

And what I would like was finally getting another taste of her, of a body that I hadn't been able to stop thinking about since I got back from Miami. I really didn't want to wait another day. I wanted her right now. On top of my desk. With her pussy rubbing against the glass, so her wetness would leave a mark that I could lick off when we were done.

Shit was changing between us.

She was no longer just a girl I'd brought home from the bar and fucked. We'd been talking every day, and we'd video-chatted —something I didn't even do with my goddamn family.

During this visit, I had a feeling I'd have to be more open with her. She'd want to know about my past. My last name. Where I worked. And that meant I'd have to tell her I wasn't a practicing attorney even though I kept my license active.

I'd have to tell her the truth—that I worked in the industry, that one of the things holding me back was her age, that I just wasn't sure if I was the right guy for her.

That coming on to her had nothing to do with signing her to The Agency.

There were agents at our old office in LA who would have done that—hooked up with potential clients to get them under contract. James's agent was one of those people.

I wasn't.

I didn't need to give someone my cock to get them signed.

I just hoped James believed that.

Industry people were guarded, cautious, because everyone wanted a piece of them.

The piece I wanted had nothing to do with her career.

There was a knock on my door. Before I could call out and ask whom it was, Jack, Max, and Scarlett walked in, each taking a seat in a chair in front of my desk. Whoever was in town and at the office usually tried to meet up at the end of each day. My office was the meeting ground since I stocked the most booze.

Scarlett handed us each a piece of paper that showed the new revenue totals, broken down by department. Now that Smith had officially joined our company and BMW was a done deal, I was in the lead.

I set the paper down on my desk and said, "Got anything to say, Jack?"

He shrugged as he continued to stare at the sheet.

"Why are you suddenly so quiet?" I asked him, winking at Scarlett. "The last time we talked about this, you had a whole lot of shit to say. Maybe you're just trying to calculate how many million I'm ahead of you? Here, let me help. It's about twelve, and by the time my team processes all of their pending contracts, we'll be over fifteen."

"You got me." Jack put his hands in the air. "Fair and square. There's no way Max or I will get even close to that number."

"Fucking-A, Brett, you killed it," Max said. "How the hell did you keep us from finding out about Smith?"

"My team knows how to keep a secret."

Both guys looked at Scarlett.

"What did he bribe you with?" Jack asked her.

She straightened her jacket and crossed her legs, trying to look innocent when she was far from it. "I have no idea what you're talking about."

When I'd come to her with the idea of keeping the guys in the dark, she'd told me she'd process the contracts herself, so her team wouldn't rat us out. That wasn't Scarlett's job; she was just doing me a favor, so I'd offered to give her half of the bet.

She didn't want it.

What she didn't know was that she was getting all of it.

And, because I knew she wouldn't take the cash, I was going to buy her something with it that she couldn't return.

"Bullshit," Max said. "You've been in on this the whole time."

"Max, that would mean I was choosing a favorite, and you know I love you all equally."

She played them so well.

"Pay up," I said to Jack and Max.

"I'll bring the cash in tomorrow," Max whined.

"Same," Jack added.

I went over to the bar in the back of my office. I took out four tumblers from the cabinet and poured several fingers' worth in each one. Then, I carried them back to my desk and handed them out as I said, "Are any of you going to LA this week?"

"I'll be there the day after tomorrow," Max said. "Why? You need something?"

Fuck.

Two of Max's clients had concerts in the LA area this week, so I'd had a feeling he'd be headed that way, too.

"I need you to sleep in a hotel for the nights you're going to be there."

All eyes were now on me.

The Agency owned the condo in LA where we all stayed whenever we were in town. We'd bought a place with four bedrooms, so it was large enough to house all of us if we ever needed to be there at the same time.

A smile came over Max's face as he set his glass on top of the desk and leaned against it to get closer to me. "Tell me, Brett, why do I need to stay somewhere else? Are you bringing someone there you don't want me to meet?"

That was obvious.

And anyone in this room could answer that question.

If James and I were in a relationship or I didn't mind the whole world finding out that she and I were fucking, I'd just stay at her place. But the paparazzi were camped outside her goddamn driveway, and the second I pulled into it, we'd be outed.

"Listen..." I paused for a second, thinking of the right way to say this. They were going to give me so much shit about her age and dump on me so hard for robbing the cradle, and I didn't want to hear it. But, since the blows were going to be unavoidable, I had to just get it over with. "I've been talking to—"

I was cut off by the sound of an alert coming through everyone's phones.

Jack and Max were the first ones to look at their screens.

"Oh, man," Max said.

"Dude, are you fucking serious?" Jack gasped.

Scarlett lifted her cell off her lap. As I watched her read the screen, I sat back in my chair and sipped my scotch, appreciating that I now had more time to figure out how I was going to tell them.

"She's the last person I expected to do something like this," Scarlett said.

"Whom are you talking about?" I asked, knowing they'd tell me, so I wouldn't have to dig in my pocket to get my phone.

She looked up, our eyes connecting. "James Ryne has a sex tape."

My fingers squeezed the fucking glass so tight, I thought it was going to shatter in my hand. "What did you just say?"

Jack and Max were staring too hard at the screen, their mouths open, eyes so goddamn wide that I wanted to punch all four back into their sockets.

"The man is yet to be identified," Scarlett said, "but the woman is definitely James."

James has a fucking sex tape?

I reached across the desk and yanked the phone out of Scarlett's hand.

"Hey!" she shouted as I took it from her. "Give that back."

I ignored her, gripping the cell in my palm, reading the headline that was at the top of her phone.

BREAKING NEWS:

JAMES RYNE AND AN UNIDENTIFIED MAN STAR IN A SEX TAPE.

AMERICA'S SWEETHEART IS NOW AMERICA'S SULTRESS.

Rage.

That was all I could feel.

It was coming in through my pores and making my entire body shake.

I wanted to take all of their phones, drop them in my trash, and set the motherfuckers on fire.

But, since I couldn't, since that would make things too obvious, I looked back at the screen and kept reading.

JAMES RYNE, EIGHTEEN-YEAR-OLD STAR OF THE RECENTLY RELEASED *WINTER'S FORGIVEN*, AND AN UNIDENTIFIED MAN HAVE BEEN CAUGHT HAVING SEXUAL RELATIONS. RYNE IS CALLED BY NAME SEVERAL TIMES THROUGHOUT THE SIXTY-TWO-MINUTE VIDEO, AND CLOSE-UP SHOTS OF HER FACE MORE THAN PROVE IT'S AMERICA'S SWEETHEART. RYNE WAS PREVIOUSLY IN A FIVE-YEAR RELATIONSHIP WITH ABEL CURRY, WHOM SHE MET ON THE SET OF *LET IT GO*. RYNE AND CURRY CONFIRMED THE END OF THEIR RELATIONSHIP SIX MONTHS AGO, AND RYNE HASN'T BEEN LINKED TO ANYONE SINCE THEN. REPS FROM RYNE'S CAMP HAVE YET TO RESPOND.

STORY STILL DEVELOPING...

I set Scarlett's phone on the desk and pushed back in my seat, staring at the empty glass of scotch. I would need ten more fingers' worth to calm me down, or my fist would be going through one of these walls.

"Wow," Max said, his eyes still on his screen.

I could only imagine what he was wowing about.

I reached toward the edge of my desk and clamped it between my fucking fingers to stop myself from grabbing it out of his hand.

If they saw my anger, they'd know.

If I said anything about the sex tape, I wouldn't be able to hold back my feelings, and they'd know then, too.

"Holy fuck," Jack said.

My teeth ground together while I watched them stare at the video of the girl I'd been thinking about nonstop.

Of the girl I was supposed to be with tomorrow.

Of the girl who had been fucking some other guy this week.

7

JAMES

Me: We need to talk.

I WAITED for the bubbles to appear on Brett's side of the message, but they never did. At least, not in the five minutes I'd been waiting for them. And they didn't within the next ten minutes either.

He always responded within thirty minutes.

Always.

So, that was how long I'd wait.

But thirty minutes came.

And went.

Forty-seven minutes.

An hour and twelve.

Now, I knew he'd seen the video.

Me: You there?

Another hour passed.

I couldn't move.

I couldn't leave the inside of my closet.

There weren't any windows in here, so they couldn't see my tears. They couldn't hear my screams.

It used to just be the paparazzi I hid from.

Now, it was the whole world.

Everyone thought they knew me because they'd seen me naked.

They knew nothing.

I would kill right now to have the warmth from my mother's hug, the feeling of her arms around me. I would do anything to have my father's hand rubbing my back. But they were gone, killed in a car crash when I was fifteen.

Without them, the only thing that would ease some of this pain was the sound of Brett's reply.

Maybe he hadn't seen the video. Maybe he'd been in court all day. In meetings. Playing golf. He hadn't seen my text because maybe his phone was in the locker room at the gym, but now, he was walking in to shower, and he would hear it ringing and answer.

Maybe. Oh God, maybe.

I opened the call log, hit his name, and waited for it to connect.

One ring.

Then...voice mail.

I didn't make it past one.

He couldn't even let me have two rings.

I hung up.

I didn't want him to hear me crying in a message.

So, I opened his text box and typed.

Me: Please call me back.

I looked above me at the racks of clothes. They hung around

the inside perimeter of my closet, stopping for a large shoe area and a case for purses and then wrapping around the rest of the room. I was in a corner, on the floor, a section of dresses hanging over me. I reached up and twisted the fabric around my fist. The silk felt cool against my skin. The wool felt scratchy. The velvet almost stuck to me.

Silk, wool, velvet.

Silk, wool, velvet.

My chest was pounding. There was an ache in my head, like a lightning bolt, that shot through my skull every few seconds.

Why?

"Why!" I shouted. "Why did this happen to me?"

I twisted and twisted and twisted and pulled with every bit of strength I had.

Hangers snapped.

Dresses ripped.

Metal banged on the hardwood floor around me.

I didn't care.

I felt nothing, except silk, wool, and velvet.

I picked it up in handfuls, setting it on top of me until I was completely covered. Until the only thing left was my face.

I filled my hands and dumped the rest over my head.

I wanted darkness.

I wanted it to swallow me.

8

BRETT

I LEFT my car at the office, too fucking buzzed to drive it to my place, and had the company driver give me a lift home. When I got inside my condo, I dropped my briefcase at the door, grabbed a bottle of scotch from the bar and my tablet from the counter, and collapsed on the couch.

I didn't know how I'd made it through the last few hours while the guys watched some more of the tape, and Scarlett had eyed me as I tried to keep my fists calm.

She knew me too well.

She always observed, unlike the other two.

I was sure she'd call my ass out soon.

Especially since I'd lied to Max, and I knew she'd seen right through it. I'd told him that an email came through, and I had to cancel my trip to LA. He must have forgotten about the hotel I'd asked him to get because he hadn't brought it up again. Regardless, I wasn't getting on that fucking plane.

While I'd sat in my office, the guys watching some of the video, I'd felt every goddamn minute that passed. I'd had to force myself not to tear the phones out of their fingers.

Knowing they had seen James naked made me fucking crazy.

Knowing another guy had had his hands on her skin and his cock in her pussy made me even crazier.

I liked her.

I liked her a hell of a lot more than I wanted to admit.

So, why the hell was I torturing myself by putting my tablet on my lap with the celebrity alert on the goddamn screen?

I had to watch it.

I had to see her with my own eyes before I reacted.

I unscrewed the bottle of scotch and swallowed down several mouthfuls, resting it on my knee while I clicked the video link at the bottom of the article.

Advertising popped up. Those fuckers were probably spending five grand a click to have their product appear before the soon-to-be most-viewed sex tape in the world.

I had to watch the ad for ten seconds before it closed, and I could get James's video to load.

It opened with a single shot.

One that made the scotch churn in my stomach.

I shot back several more swallows and continued to stare at James on her knees with those pouty lips wrapped around a cock.

Jesus Christ.

I had to keep watching; the intro could just be a series of Photoshopped pictures.

But then the video began to play, and James walked out of a door that looked like a bathroom, wearing a pair of red lace panties and a matching bra, moving slowly across the carpet. There was a guy sitting on the end of the bed, naked. His face was blurred, making it impossible to see his features or anything that would identify him.

"Get over here," he said in a voice I could tell had been altered, "and get on your fucking knees."

I gripped the neck of the bottle as she put her hands on his thighs and slid to the floor, her mouth opening to take in his crown.

I can't fucking believe I'm watching this.

She took it fast, deep, and played with his balls after he ordered her to. And, just as she established a rhythm, he pulled her by the hair, lifted her off the floor, and tossed her on the bed. He wasn't gentle when he yanked off her panties or downed the straps of her bra instead of unhooking it in the back.

He didn't kiss her tits.

He didn't finger-fuck her pussy.

He put a condom on, flipped her onto her stomach, and spit on her cunt. Pumping his cock a few times, he slid in behind her and rammed it in.

She moaned.

It wasn't the same noise that she'd made with me.

Not even fucking close.

The sound was to please him.

He told her to get up on her knees and stick her ass in the air. She did.

He told her to move up higher, so he could pump her deeper. She did.

He wasn't trying to make her feel good. He didn't give a fuck about her.

He wanted to come.

"James," he groaned. "James fucking Ryne."

He turned her onto her back so that her profile now faced the camera. She rolled her head to the side and looked straight at me.

Her lips parted.

Her eyes were full of pain.

The world would think that was how she looked when an orgasm was building in her body. Her sounds were convincing enough.

I knew better.

I knew what she looked like when she came, and that wasn't it.

"James," he groaned again, giving her fast thrusts, squeezing her tit like he was testing a goddamn piece of fruit. "Oh God, James."

He shook.

He stilled.

He climbed off.

He walked to the bathroom.

James stayed on her back for a little while, appearing as though she were catching her breath. When she finally sat up, she spread her legs for just a second before she tucked them against her chest and wrapped her arms around them.

In the short amount of time that her legs were open, I saw what I had been looking for.

The small, dark freckle on the inside of her thigh.

It was her.

That mark had confirmed it.

There was still fifty-eight minutes left of the video. That meant they'd had sex more than once, and if this guy could only keep it in for four minutes, then there were several more sessions like the bullshit I'd just witnessed.

I tossed the tablet across my couch.

I'd believed her. The flirting, the begging me to come visit, the wanting of what I could give her body. So, my assistant had rearranged my whole schedule to get me to LA as fast as possible, I'd reached out to one of my favorite chefs, and I had been seconds away from outing myself to all my friends...for nothing.

Because, the whole time, she had been out fucking another dude.

I pulled my phone from my pocket and looked at the screen. There were texts from the guys and Scarlett, wanting me to show up at the bar they were at. There were messages from clients, from my team and support staff.

I ignored them all.

I clicked on James's last text. She'd been blowing up my phone for a few hours. She'd even called, and I'd sent her straight to voice mail. I hadn't been ready to talk yet.

I was now.

> *Me: What the fuck did I just watch?*
> *James: Brett, I'm so sorry.*
> *Me: I'm done.*
> *James: We need to talk about this. You can't be done. We have something here; you know we do. Just hear me out; let me tell you what happened.*
> *James: Brett...*
> *James: Brett, please.*
> *James: Please talk to me.*
> *James: Don't do this to me.*

I left my cell on the couch and stood. Holding the bottle like it was a leash, I moved through the living room and toward the master suite.

I didn't want to see another word that came across the screen of that phone.

I didn't want to send another call to voice mail.

I was a man of my word, and I'd just given her my last one.

9

JAMES

"LISTEN TO ME, James, this is exactly what you need," Eve said as she squeezed my hand, walking me through the front door of a friend's house.

A friend who had promised Eve that she would only have a few people over, and it would be a quiet and relaxing night.

That was all I could handle.

Because, for the first time in three days, I had actually left my closet.

In the time I'd spent in there, not only had I learned my Dior contract was canceled, but I'd also lost endorsement deals for a shampoo and conditioner, perfume, and teeth whitening kit. It was where I'd been told my two upcoming movies in pre-production dropped me, and they were recasting my role.

My entire world was exploding, and I could do nothing to stop it.

While that had all been happening, my manager, attorney, agent, and publicist had all stood around the island in my closet—the one covered in my jewelry and sunglasses—and told me how I should move forward, what statement was going to be released, and the things I needed to say to the police whenever I met with them to press charges.

I hadn't heard any of it.

Because I had been on the floor, buried underneath all my clothes, reading the vile things that people were saying about me online. The pictures they'd created, the memes, the GIFs—it all made me sick.

It made me hurt.

It made me want to give up.

Eve couldn't take another second of me being in the closet. So, after my team had left, she'd pulled me out of the clothes pile, stripped off the outfit I'd been wearing since the Dior shoot, and put me in the shower. She'd stood by the glass door and told me to wash my hair and scrub my body, or she wouldn't let me out. When I'd finished both, she had gotten me ready and handed me a straw that she'd stuck in a glass of wine.

She'd told me to suck.

I had.

A total of three glasses.

Man, was I drunk.

And it felt good.

And I knew everyone who was at my friend's house, which was the biggest relief because Eve could tell the small group to lay off the questions and that I'd talk about it when I was ready.

They all seemed to understand.

So, we sat around and played drinking games. I listened to them tell stories about their families and the trips they were planning, and I laughed for the first time in days.

But, after two stories in a row about botched boob jobs, I looked down at my cup, and it was empty.

I needed it full.

I needed the alcohol to continue taking all this pain away.

Pushing myself off the couch, I rushed into the kitchen and

saw so many bottles on the counter. I chose a pretty green one and a sexy red one, pouring them in together, and I topped it with some juice I'd found in the fridge.

As I was mixing it with my finger, I heard Eve say, "*Jaaames.*"

"Eve," I replied and turned around, throwing an arm across her shoulders. "This is the most perfect night. Such a good call on bringing me here."

If I kept telling myself that, I would believe it. I would feel normal. I would forget what was really happening and just focus on my friends.

"Told ya, bitch." Her fingers clenched mine. "Now, let's go have more *fuuun.*" She released one of my hands but still clung to the other and dragged me through the kitchen.

"Eve," I panted, trying not to fall in my heels, "I'm going to spill my drink."

She gazed at me from over her shoulder and said, "We can't have that now, can we?"

I kneed her in the butt, and she laughed.

When we got to the living room, she climbed on the back of the couch, and from there, she jumped onto the buffet table.

"Turn on the music," she said, pointing at one of the girls. "Let's dance."

The music started, and the lights dimmed. Suddenly, everyone was on their feet and dancing. Eve kept calling out my name while I was shaking it with the other girls, and I finally turned toward her.

"Get up here, woman," she demanded.

I kicked off my heels and got on top of the couch, the same way she had, and I jumped to the table. I squealed as I landed, my foot sliding on the wood, almost taking the both of us out. But Eve caught me and steadied my body, and then neither of us could stop laughing.

The alcohol made the minutes blend together. It made the

faces around me seem like they were all smiling. It made my body flow seamlessly from one beat to the next every time a new song came on. It made the group of people who had gathered below us not seem out of place even though they hadn't been here when I first arrived.

"Give me your butt," Eve said. She stuck hers out and waited for me to grind mine against it. *"Yaaas."* She laughed. "Get it, girl."

We both turned around to face each other again, our arms rising above our heads, fingers linked.

"God, I love this music," she said, our movements matching, our hips swaying, our hands swishing.

"Me, too," I agreed just as a guy jumped on the table on the other side of her.

He was dancing behind her, and I was dancing in front of her.

When the song changed, I heard a girl say, "Why the fuck would she let a guy tape her during sex? Didn't she learn anything from watching reality TV?"

I knew the voice had come from somewhere nearby, but there were so many people standing in the living room now—girls I'd never seen before, guys who weren't familiar at all.

I grabbed Eve's arm and whispered in her ear, "Who are all these people? And where did they come from?"

She glanced around the room and shrugged. "I have no idea, but don't worry about them."

I tried to follow her advice, but then I heard, "She's obviously trying to get into porn."

"Nah," another guy said. "She just wanted the whole world to see her naked."

Oh my God.

"Don't be so hard on her, guys," a different voice said. "She does have one hell of a body, and if I looked like that, I'd be showing it off, too."

I couldn't place the voices or see where they were coming from. There were just too many people in here.

"Fucking pathetic—that's what she is."

Don't they understand this wasn't my fault?

That I didn't do this to myself?

That I've been working since I was thirteen to get to where I am?

Had it been my choice, I certainly wouldn't have ruined my career and reputation over a sex tape.

"Eve—" My voice halted when I felt my back pocket vibrate. From the amount of times it had gone off, I knew it had to be a phone call. Hoping it might be Brett, I pulled it out and saw my agent's name on the screen.

"Eve," I continued and turned her around to face me. "Help me down. I have to take this call."

She gave me her hand, and I used it to step onto the back of the couch. Then, I released her to rush down the cushion and weave through all the people to get to the hallway where I opened one of the closed doors.

"Hello?" I answered and shut the door behind me.

"Are you at a fucking party right now?"

There wasn't any music in here, and I was alone.

How does he know?

"Yes," I said. "But it's—"

"I don't want to hear what you're about to say. I'm calling to tell you, I'm resigning as your agent. And I just got off the phone with your publicist, and she's doing the same. Official resignations are in your inbox."

Done?

No.

Brett was done.

Brett had abandoned me when I needed his voice the most.

My agent and publicist couldn't do that to me, too.

"I need your help. I—"

"I can't help you, James," he said, cutting me off. "Best of luck."

"Hey, wait—"

I stopped talking when the phone went dead.

I set it on my palm, staring at the screen, willing it to light up with my agent's name.

Call me back.

Text me.

Please.

Seconds passed. Minutes. The only things that came through were more social media tags, more pictures and memes and GIFs.

More words I didn't want to read.

Everyone was done with me.

I was done.

The room started spinning, my stomach hurting more after each twirl. My body was so heavy, and my chest felt like it was going to crack.

I had to get out of here.

I went into the hallway where there were even more people than before. I felt their stares as I passed them. Their skin, their shoulders, their hands, their clothes—it all brushed against me.

"Take me doggy-style," one of them said.

Their lips were close. Their voices stung.

They were mocking what I had said in the video.

"Fuck me harder," another person blurted out.

"Stop," I whispered, knowing they couldn't hear me but still needing to say it.

"You have the sweetest cunt," a guy said, his breath on the back of my ear. "Let me show you what it feels like to have a real cock inside you."

I wiggled, trying to get his mouth away from me. Those movements brought me to the other side of the hallway where someone stepped on my bare foot, causing me to jerk forward and slam into the person in front of me.

"I want you in that red lace getup while you wrap your lips around my cock."

His hands were now on my ass, his face in my neck, and he was turning me around.

I couldn't stop him, but I tried like hell.

"I'm going to fuck you so hard."

I didn't even see what he looked like. I just pushed both hands against his chest, shoving him as hard as I could, and I stumbled backward and fell into something.

Something wooden.

A door.

I quickly opened it and closed it behind me. I leaned my back into it as I tried to find my breath.

They had all seen the video. Every one of them out there.

They knew how I sounded when I begged. When I faked an orgasm. When I got on my knees and opened my mouth and gave head.

They knew my pussy was bare.

They knew the color of my nipples.

Now, the whole world was judging me.

I couldn't handle it.

Not even realizing I was standing in the dark, I searched for a switch and flipped it on. I blinked and then a second time, the light blinding me, which only made my stomach feel worse.

There was a knock.

"Hurry up. I've gotta take a piss."

I said nothing back to him and looked around, seeing that I was in a bathroom.

A wave of heat came over me, and my mouth watered. I

darted over to the toilet and lifted the seat. Everything that had been in my belly came up. With each heave, I saw the tweets I'd been tagged in and the pictures and memes and GIFs.

Disappointment.
Unemployable.
Slut.
Whore.

I flushed, and as I went over to the sink to wash my mouth and hands, I caught a glimpse of my face. The retching had caused my makeup to run, my hair was sweaty and wild, and my eyes were bloodshot. I couldn't stop staring at my reflection, at this girl who was gazing at me, because she looked nothing like me.

Disgusted, I turned on the water, and just as I did, my phone lit up with a text.

Eve: Where the hell are you?
Me: Bathroom.
Eve: Which one?

I scanned the small room.

Me: Black-and-white-striped wallpaper.
Eve: I'll find you.

I washed my hands and dried them, and then I held on to the edge of the sink, keeping my face toward the door so that I wouldn't catch my reflection. Before I knew it, there was a knock.

"James, it's Eve. Let me in," she said.

I reached for the knob, hitting the small button that released the lock. "Close it," I said once she came in. "Lock it, too."

She immediately came over and hugged me. "Did you get sick? It smells like puke in here."

I pulled away. Her skin was too clammy, and it was making me hot again.

"Eve, my agent just fired me, and so did my publicist. People are saying the most horrible things about me out there. I can't..." I tried to take a breath. "I can't be here anymore."

"Oh, honey, what did your agent say?"

"He said the same thing as Brett. He's done." My chest was rising so fast, and my stomach was still so tight. My feet didn't at all feel steady on the floor. "I have to go home."

"Someone said the paparazzi are outside. They're covering the whole front lawn and driveway."

My belly churned and flipped.

Oh my God.

"They want a picture of me, don't they?"

"I'm afraid so."

I couldn't go out there. They'd already gotten enough of me, and I refused to give them more.

"Where did all these people come from? I thought this was supposed to be a quiet girls' night?"

"I don't know," she said. "They're not supposed to be here."

"What am I going to do, Eve?"

She shook her head, her hands playing with the front of my hair. I could smell the liquor on her breath. I could see her teetering on her feet.

She was drunker than me.

"I'm going to call my manager," I said.

He was the only other person I had, the only one who hadn't left me.

Her face lit up. "Yes, good idea. Tim can help. I know he can."

I grabbed my phone, found his number, and pressed it, holding the speaker to my ear.

"James," he said after the first ring, "is everything all right?"

I could tell he'd been sleeping, and I'd woken him up.

"No, everything is definitely not all right." I told him about the phone call with my agent and the things people had been saying to me at this party and how the paparazzi were waiting outside and wouldn't leave until they got a photo. "Tim, I need help. I don't know how to get out of here." I didn't know when I had started crying, but tears were falling, my lips were soaked, and I couldn't catch my breath. "I don't know how to fix this. It's all falling apart, everything, my whole life, and it's just getting worse."

Eve reached for my other hand and squeezed it, catching my tears before they fell down my cheeks.

"I have an idea," he said.

"Thank God," Eve and I replied at the same time.

"I'm coming to get you. Send me the address. I'll be there as soon as I can."

"I'm texting it over right now," Eve said. She grabbed the phone from me, her fingers typing on the screen. When she finished, she set it on the counter and turned back to me. "He's never let you down in all the years he's worked for you. He's going to make this better."

I listened to her.

I tried to believe her.

But I didn't know how anyone could fix this or how things could ever get better.

And, no matter what any of them did, they couldn't get Brett to come back.

"Don't leave me," I said. "Wait until Tim gets here, and then go back to the party. I don't want to be alone."

She tightly held me and smiled. "I'm not going anywhere, babe."

And she didn't.

She stayed in that bathroom until Tim called. When I

answered, he asked me to put Eve on the phone, and I listened while he told her his plan. As she hung up, she took off the small jacket she had on over her tube top, and she put it on my head. Then, she took a bath towel off the rack and wrapped it over my shoulders.

"I'm going to walk you out," she said. "The whole time, we have to make sure you're completely covered. Tim's parked right out back, so we only have to get you from the door to his car. Got it?"

"Okay."

"I'd kiss you if you didn't reek of puke."

I wanted to smile and laugh, but I couldn't.

She made sure I was ready, and then she opened the bathroom door and led me into the hallway. Behind the towel and jacket, I could only see my feet, so I had to rely on her steering me through the house.

It was so hot under these layers.

And there were more comments and laughter and people banging into me.

I tried to ignore it all.

I tried to hold my breath.

I tried to focus on something other than what was happening.

And, finally, I felt a burst of air, and I knew we'd made it outside.

"That's her!" I heard someone yell. "That's James Ryne!"

I felt a rush—feet on the pavement, the shuttering of cameras, questions and accusations being thrown at me.

"Back up!" Eve screamed. "Give us some room!"

Someone new grabbed my arm and said, "I've got her."

It was Tim's voice, Tim's grip, Tim's feet that I saw close to mine.

"I'm coming with you guys," Eve said.

I was afraid to respond because I didn't want the paparazzi to hear my voice.

Tim took care of that for me when he said, "Not tonight. I've got her."

He helped me climb up and shut the door behind me, and I was finally in the back seat of his SUV.

I heard another door open and close, and he said, "Keep your head covered until I get us out of here."

As we began to move, I tucked my body into the corner, pressing one shoulder into the seat and another into the door, and I tried to relax my heart that felt like it was beating out of my chest.

"Almost there," he said.

There was pounding on the windows and more on the doors and flashes that lit up the bottom of the towel.

I felt the SUV jerk when Tim stepped on the gas, and finally, he said, "Okay, you're safe."

I let the jacket fall to my lap, and I took in deep breaths of the air-conditioning.

"Thank you," I said, resting my face on the cool glass of the window, my eyes closing as my temperature started to come down.

"I'm going to tell you my plan."

"Please don't." I didn't even open my eyes. They hurt too much for that. And so did my ears. I just wanted silence. "I trust you, Tim."

I felt us turn and come to a stop, and then we were moving again.

"You need to know, I ordered us a plane, and we'll be flying out in an hour."

I adjusted my face to find more coldness on the glass. "Okay."

"Don't you want to know where we're going?"

I hadn't slept since the celebrity alert went out. I hadn't even shut my eyes. Not even once.

But here, in Tim's car, with my face on the window and the air-conditioning blowing on me and the jacket and towel acting as a blanket, I felt sleepy.

"Just help me, Tim. That's all I care about."

10

BRETT

Scarlett: Are you awake?
Me: No.
Scarlett: Then, why are you answering me?
Me: Because you're fucking texting me.
Scarlett: Can you come open your door? My hand hurts from knocking.

I EXITED out of the text and checked the time. It was past two in the morning.

I didn't remember falling asleep, but I was on top of my bed, still in my clothes, my computer on my lap, and a half-bottle of scotch lying next to me. There was another one on the nightstand from the night before.

I'd spent the entire day in meetings and had so much work to catch up on. So, when the guys and Scarlett had left to go to a concert that Max's client was headlining, I'd bailed and come home to get shit done.

I walked to the front door and pulled it open, not even

waiting to see her face before I turned around and headed for the couch.

I heard her follow me, coming in from the other side of the sectional to take the seat beside me.

She slid off her heels and put her feet on the ottoman, turning her head toward me. "You missed a fun night."

"I'm pissed I had to skip it. I'm fucking drowning in work right now."

"I know. I've never seen your team submit this many contracts before." She tossed her purse a few cushions down. "But that's not why I'm here. We need to talk."

I sank down even further, resting the back of my head into the top cushion and crossing my feet next to hers. "What do you want to talk about?"

She waited until I looked at her and said, "James Ryne."

My chest started to pound, and I had to wait a few seconds before I responded, "There's nothing to say about her."

"I came to your house at two in the morning. We're going to talk about her because you need to."

I said nothing.

"Fine then, I'll do the talking, Brett. You know I'm good at that."

"Jesus Christ."

"I'm going to guess that you met James during your last trip to LA. Probably at the Chateau Marmont because I know that's where you and Smith were supposed to talk, and I know you didn't end up meeting with Tony across town, so you were busy with someone. I'm thinking that someone was James. You two spent the night together, and then you flew back the next morning." She leaned forward and slid all her hair onto one shoulder. "When I saw you that night at the bar, it was James you were texting back and forth with. If you plan on denying it, don't. I saw her name on your phone. Anyway, I know you feel something for her, and she makes you happy. I saw that as well over the past few weeks. And then I saw your face when the celebrity alert came through. I thought you were going to start throwing punches."

"I almost did."

"Was I close to getting it all right?"

I turned my head to look at her. "You're in the wrong fucking career."

"It's because I'm a woman, and I have good instincts, but I would make one hell of a PI, I know." She tapped her thumb into my arm. "Is it because of her age? Is that why you didn't tell us?"

I reached up, pulling at the collar of my T-shirt. "I haven't told you because there isn't anything to say about it. James and I fucked. We talked on the phone for a month. I was going to see her in LA, and when the alert came out, I canceled my trip. End of story."

"Stop avoiding my question."

I turned my head away from her and sighed. "Jesus, Scarlett, I was on the front page of *Miami Magazine* as the most eligible bachelor in the city. She's America's sweetheart. She's eighteen. I have no fucking business getting involved with her."

"But you like her. I can tell. So, obviously, her age didn't matter when you spent the night with her."

"I gave myself a one-fuck pass."

"Then, what would you call this week?"

I gritted my teeth together. "A fuck that never happened. We're done here."

I went to lean up, and she stopped me by putting her hand on my chest.

"We're *almost* done. Do you know anything about the video?"

"No."

"Well, did you give her a chance to tell you about it?"

"No, Scarlett, I didn't call her and ask her to give me every fucking detail about the dude who was fucking her. And don't tell me I should have because the thought of that makes me want to throw this ottoman out the window and watch it fall down the thirty-five stories."

She pushed against me a little harder. "You're a stubborn prick, you know that?"

"I know I didn't get to where I am because I'm a nice guy. I know the chick I was talking to was banging some other dude and just so happened to get busted." I bit into my bottom lip. "I should have gone to meet Tony. Taking her back to my place was a fucking mistake."

"Maybe. Or maybe it wasn't. But I think you should talk to her about it."

"Here we go with all the, *You're making the biggest mistake of your life, Brett. You'll regret this, Brett.*"

Now, it was her turn to sit up, but it was only to get a better view of my face. "I think you'll regret it, yes, because I don't think you're giving her a chance."

"I don't want to hear her apologize. We weren't together. We weren't anything. There was no reason she shouldn't have hooked up with him."

"Then, why are you upset?"

"Because I fucking liked her, and it's bullshit that—"

A sound came through my phone, a ringtone that was reserved for celebrity alerts. I didn't want to fucking look, but it could be about a client, and that was why I took my phone out of my pocket.

TABLES, DANCING, GRINDING, OH MY!
ISN'T JAMES RYNE HAVING A GRAND OLD TIME?

I held the phone out, so Scarlett could see the screen, and I clicked on the headline. A picture of James appeared. She was standing on a table with the girl she had been with at the bar. James's arms were in the air, her knees bent.

She was dancing.

Grinding.

And she was smiling so goddamn hard.

"Can you fucking believe this?" I snapped. "I'm torn up because America's sweetheart has a sex tape that's ruining her career, and she's out there, celebrating."

Scarlett shook her head. "Why isn't her team advising against this? Doesn't she know this is making it worse? That all the attention she's bringing to herself is only fueling the media more."

"It's not my problem." When her eyes softened, I added, "Just drop it. I'm done. I'm not talking about it any more. It was a month—that's all it was—and I'm over it."

11

BRETT

I RETURNED to the office the following morning after only a few hours of sleep, arriving before my team so that I could get more work done. Before I came in, I'd spent an hour hitting the bag at the gym. Sixty fucking minutes, and I still hadn't gotten all the anger out.

I'd never been so wrong about a girl.

And last night's celebrity alert had only made it worse. If there were a chance I would have called her before, there was no fucking chance now.

I turned my computer on, and the emails started to come through. My clients filming in Europe were just leaving the set and sending over documents that I'd needed them to sign. The European brands were getting in touch to inquire about some new contracts. New York was already filming, and there were set issues and no-shows. And I had a client complaining about things that hadn't been delivered at their photo shoot. And, as I was looking at images of one of my actors who had gotten hurt on set, there was a knock at my door.

"Come in," I said, glancing up from my computer screen,

knowing it was the guys and Scarlett, meeting about The Agency's sixth-anniversary party that we were hosting in a few months.

They all walked in with coffees in their hands and took their seats around my desk.

Scarlett hadn't told the guys about our conversation last night. I was sure she hadn't even told them she came to my place. That was how we all worked; some shit was meant to be shared between all four of us, and some just wasn't.

"Dude, you missed a hell of a show last night," Max said.

"I heard it was good," I replied. "Sorry I had to bail. I just had too much to do."

"You know I understand that," Max said, picking up one of the contracts on my desk to check out the first few pages.

"How's this morning been so far?" Scarlett asked me, looking as tired as I felt.

I shook my head. "Fucking crazy. You wouldn't even believe some of the bullshit going on. I might need to fly to New York tonight; I have a client in the hospital."

"Which one?" Jack asked.

"Larry," I said. "He fell off a balcony when they were filming on the second story of a hotel. Broken collarbone, both wrists shattered, and he needs surgery immediately."

"Jesus Christ," Max said. "Have you heard from his family?"

"They're flying there now."

"Let me know if he's all right," Jack said.

"Let all of us know," Scarlett said.

I nodded and heard another knock on my door. "Come in," I said a second time.

My assistant popped her head in.

"What's up?"

She looked at the guys and at Scarlett before her attention

turned toward me. "Sorry to interrupt, but you have some visitors."

"Who?"

"James Ryne and her manager, Tim Thomas, are downstairs in reception. Since they weren't listed on your schedule, the receptionist wouldn't send them upstairs, so she called me. They know they don't have an appointment, but they're requesting to see you as soon as possible."

My teeth ground so fucking hard, I heard my jaw crack. "What do they want?"

"They wouldn't say when the receptionist asked. But, from my understanding, they just flew in and came straight here from the airport."

I was holding the armrests of my chair, squeezing them with all my strength, waiting for them to snap off.

Why would James come here? All the way to Miami? With her fucking manager?

It had nothing to do with what had happened between us, or she wouldn't have brought Tim.

She had come because she needed my help, or Tim was the one who had pushed for it. Either way, she'd figured out I was an agent and not a practicing attorney.

It didn't matter. There was no way in hell I was going to give my assistant the okay to send them upstairs.

I was done with James Ryne.

"They don't have an appointment. Tell them I'm busy," I said.

"Hold on," Jack said to my assistant before he looked at me. "Are you fucking crazy? So what if she doesn't have an appointment? She flew all the way here to talk to you, and you're just going to send that kind of business away? Do you know how much money that girl makes every year?"

"Made," I corrected him.

From what I'd read this morning, she'd lost all of her contracts and both upcoming movies.

No one wanted to hire her.

"With your help, she'll get all of it back," Max said.

He'd obviously read the reports, too.

It was hard not to.

James was the headline on every fucking news source right now.

"I'm not interested," I told them.

Max looked at Scarlett and said, "What's his problem? Has he lost his goddamn mind?"

Her eyes shifted over to me, and I knew she was in a rough place. She wanted like hell to tear into me, but she'd never do that in front of the guys, not when they didn't know about James and me.

"Brett, if you don't take the meeting, I'm going to," Jack said.

I tried to hold my anger in. "No, you're not."

"Like hell I'm not," he said. "That girl needs some fucking help, and I don't know why you're not willing to do it, but I will. Remember, the reason we walked away from those assholes in LA—like the one who represents her—is because, no matter how hard things got, we would never turn our back on a client. So, at the very least, someone from this office is going to give her some guidance. If you want to pass, then I'll make an exception, and I'll work hybrid until I get her back on her feet."

I stood, moving over to the bar, realizing it was far too fucking early to pour anything to drink. They were all watching me. Even my assistant.

My interest in James was becoming more obvious every goddamn second.

"You wouldn't do that," I told Jack. "You wouldn't cross teams. None of us would ever do that."

"Brett, please—"

"Scarlett," Max said, cutting her off, "you're going to be too nice. Let me take a stab at him." Max glared at me. "You're right; we don't cross teams, and none of us have ever gone hybrid, but we've also never been in a situation where someone needs our help, and they're willing to come all the way here to get it. I'll admit, acting isn't a language I speak, certainly not fluently like you. But I'm not going to turn the girl down either. So, whatever you have against James Ryne, get over it, and get your shit together."

My jaw clenched, and my fingers gripped the bar.

I fucking hated that my friends were getting involved in this. I wanted them to stay out of it; I wanted this decision to be mine.

I wanted James to get back in her plane and return to where she belonged.

"You've certainly taken on harder cases than a sex tape, so what the hell is your deal?" Jack said.

My eyes moved to each of their faces as they waited for me to respond.

"Brett, just hear what they have to say," Max added.

It was the same request Scarlett had made last night.

Back then, neither of us had known that we'd be faced with this today.

And, now, here James was, right at my fucking feet.

"Send them into the conference room," I told my assistant.

And she shut the door behind her.

"I think the four of us should sit in on this meeting," Jack said.

They all glanced at me, waiting for a response.

It took me a few seconds to give them one. "Well then, by all fucking means, let's get this show on the road."

12

JAMES

THE SUV PULLED up in front of a massive mirrored building in downtown Miami and parked, the driver coming around to my side to help me out. I climbed out first and waited for Tim, and then he led me through the front door.

The lobby was a mixture of stone and shiny metal and beautiful pieces of contemporary art. Everything looked so clean and polished, even the receptionist sitting behind her desk. She smiled as we walked in, and I returned the gesture, feeling my phone vibrate in my back pocket.

I took it out, and there was a text from Eve on the screen.

"You go answer that," Tim said. "I'll take care of things here."

"You sure?"

He nodded and pointed toward the couches and chairs on the other side of the massive space. "Get comfortable. We might be here for a while."

As Tim walked over to the receptionist, I made my way to one of the couches and curled into the corner.

Eve: Where are you? I just went to your house, and you're not

there.
Me: I'm in Miami.
Eve: What? With Tim?
Me: Yep. He wants me to meet with someone who can help, I
guess.
Eve: Paparazzi are stalking your house. I almost punched one in
the face when he tried to stop me from getting in my car. Make
sure Tim brings you home, or maybe stay in a hotel for a few days.
Me: God. This is out of control. I just want it to end.
Eve: I know, babe, but you'll get through it. XO

As I looked up, Tim was sitting in one of the chairs across from me.

"Did she say how long?" I asked him.

He shook his head, so I glanced back at my phone, scrolling through my emails, finally reading the resignation letters my agent and publicist had sent.

As I thought about all the money my agent had made off me, I started to feel sick. He was such a dickhead for doing this to me. I hoped his other clients found out how much of an asshole he was, and I hoped they left him because of it.

Tossing my phone on the cushion, I noticed the receptionist was headed for us.

"Mr. Young would like me to bring you upstairs," she said as she stopped by Tim's chair.

We stood and followed her to an elevator, which took us several floors above, and then we were led to a conference room.

"Mr. Young will be in shortly," she said and closed the door.

I looked like hell. The mirror in the bathroom on the plane had confirmed that.

I had nothing with me—no change of clothes, no makeup, not even a pair of shoes to put on my feet. The flight attendant had given me some slippers and a toothbrush. At least my mouth tasted like mint, but the soft cotton slip-ons didn't give me much traction on the slick marble floors in here.

I had tried to clean myself up before we landed, combing my hair with my fingers, wiping away the excess eyeliner with some toilet paper.

I hoped whomever we were meeting wouldn't judge me on what I looked like right now.

I walked around to the far side of the table and sat in the middle, taking a glance around the room. There wasn't much to look at, just a big table, chairs, a giant logo on the wall that said *The Agency*, and some refreshments next to the door. I swiveled in my seat and turned toward the windows that overlooked the skyline of Miami.

Tim hadn't told me we were coming to Florida. I hadn't let him. We'd barely said a handful of words to each other the whole flight, as I'd slept almost the entire time. The reason I had known where we were going was from the monitors on the plane that showed our flight path.

I wasn't sure who worked in this office or what they could do to help me, but I hoped we could quickly wrap things up, so I could get right back on the plane. Brett lived in Miami. The last thing I wanted was to run into him.

In fact, I never wanted to see that man again.

I couldn't believe that I'd meant absolutely nothing to him.

That he had cut me off so easily and thrown me away.

Heartless bastard.

"I want you to be honest during this meeting," Tim said. "If you're asked about what happened during the night in Malibu, it's okay to tell the whole story."

The thought made me queasy.

He was asking me to turn vulnerable, to share those intimate moments with a complete stranger.

Just because there was a video of me having sex on the internet, showing that I could read lines and sound convincing on camera, didn't mean this wasn't hard for me.

That night in Malibu hadn't just burned me.

It had ruined me.

And here I was, once again taking a chance on someone I didn't know.

In the reflection of the windows, I saw the door open, and I heard, "Good morning."

That voice.

My hands shifted over to the armrests, each finger shaking as I squeezed the plastic between them. Goose bumps covered my skin. Air was going out much faster than it was coming in. I couldn't take a deep breath. I couldn't get it past the knot in my throat.

Mr. Young is...Brett Young?

It couldn't be.

There was no chance in hell.

But it was.

Two words was all he had said, all it had taken for me to place that voice.

And, God, that voice had done so many things to me over the past month.

I didn't want to turn around.

I didn't want to see him.

I wanted to throw myself through that door and down the stairs and head straight back to the plane.

"Tim," Brett said, his tone vibrating through my chest and straight to my toes. "It's a pleasure to see you again."

Again?

I turned toward Tim. Unable to keep it in, I shrieked, "You know him?"

I gasped when I felt Brett's stare hit my profile.

But I couldn't return the look.

It hurt way too much.

"We've met several times," Tim said. The look on his face told me he was surprised by my outburst, maybe even a little embarrassed. He glanced at Brett and said, "You, too."

How in the hell is Brett going to help me?

I tried to come up with an answer as sweat started seeping out of my pores.

There wasn't enough air in here.

I knew he was standing across from me. I could see him in my peripheral vision. And I was suffocating from his eyes. I didn't want to look at them.

"James, it's really good to see you again," Brett said.

So, this is how we're going to play it?

Unbelievable.

"I'd like to introduce you to my colleagues," Brett continued.

I hadn't realized other people had entered the room. If I glanced at them, I'd have to turn toward Brett. I didn't want that. I didn't want to see his handsome face or the suit I knew he had on or hear his words as they were spoken directly at me. All of that would soften me, and I couldn't let that happen. I was pissed at him for what he'd done.

But, at the same time, I didn't want to disappoint Tim. He was the only one who had stuck by me when everyone else left.

So, slowly, I spun the chair until my body was pointed forward, gradually lifting my head until our eyes connected.

Those big, beautiful green eyes.

Ones I'd memorized from our video chats.

Ones that were glaring at me like I had done something wrong.

It felt like all the air was being sucked out of my body.

"James, I wasn't aware that you already knew Brett," Tim said. "So, in that case, we can skip introductions, and you can meet the rest of his team."

"You're all lawyers?" I asked, looking around the table at the three other people sitting around it.

"No," the woman at the end said, "not all of us." She stood, holding out her hand, which I shook. "I'm Scarlett Davis, CFO of The Agency." She pointed at the man next to her, who had dark features but wasn't as polished as the other guys. "This is Max Graham; he runs our music division." She pointed at the next guy, who had medium-brown hair with blue eyes, the same build as Brett. "That's Jack Hunt; he's in charge of sports." Her finger moved once again. "And you already know Brett, who runs our acting department."

"I'm confused, Brett. I thought—"

"James, The Agency is a talent agency," Brett said. "The three of us guys are agents, and the four of us are partners."

Agents?

But he had told me he was an attorney.

What a fucking liar.

Brett Young, Brett Young, I repeated in my head.

Suddenly, it clicked. I'd heard his name many times before. He was a top agent, representing some of the biggest stars in the business. He had a reputation for being ruthless.

I wasn't surprised.

I'd seen that side of him the second the celebrity alert went viral.

Brett crossed his hands on top of the table, and I couldn't look away. I knew how those fingers could feel on my body. I knew that the slight sweep of his thumb could give me a quick, hard orgasm.

Those hands would never be near me again.

I had no idea how I was going to get through this meeting.

"James," Scarlett said, "why don't you tell us why you're here?"

My stare shifted off Brett's hands and moved over to Tim. He would have to answer that one. I didn't know what we were doing here or why I was still sitting in this room.

"Last night, we found out that James's agent and publicist resigned," Tim said. "Once I heard the news, I immediately thought of Brett. It was too late to reach out, so I ordered us a plane and just came straight here." Tim looked at the bastard across from me. "If anyone can fix what's been done, it's you."

Tim wants Brett to be my agent?

I was doing everything I could not to vomit the coffee I'd had on the plane.

"To explain some of James's shock," Tim added, "she didn't know we were meeting with a new talent agency or what I planned on discussing with you." He glanced back at me, and now, I wished I had let him give me more details, so I could have stopped this trip before it happened. "All of this came about rather quickly."

"To confirm, you're saying you're no longer represented?" Jack asked me.

I turned my head toward him. "No. Everyone important, except Tim, has left me."

I felt Brett's stare.

I did everything I could not to gaze in his direction. I wouldn't be able to stomach the frigid expression on his face.

"Why don't you start from the beginning?" Scarlett said. "Tell us what happened, and how the sex tape came about, and then we can go from there."

Focusing on the four other faces, still avoiding Brett's, I began to unravel the last six months of my life. "Three months ago, I got a call from Abel Curry, my ex-boyfriend. I was filming in Toronto, and he wanted me to come back to LA to move my things out of our house. While I was there, packing up, his new girlfriend, Sophia Sully, wouldn't leave me alone. She made those few hours completely miserable."

I got angry, just thinking about the things she had said to me, remembering how much of a bitch she had been, how she'd told me Abel never loved me, that she'd been fucking him for months before I caught them in bed together.

"Later that night, I was at a party, and Abel and Sophia showed up. I'd never seen them together in person, only pictures of them online. It was just awful. I swear, she laid on the PDA extra thick, just trying to upset me. And it worked."

I took a breath, but all the pain in my chest wasn't from Abel, although there was a little of that in there, too. It was from the video, it was from last night's party, it was from the coldness that Brett's stare had filled me with.

"This guy, Calvin Parker, started hitting on me, and I flirted right back. I wanted to see if I could make Abel notice and maybe a little jealous. Before I knew it, we were leaving. We headed to his hotel in Malibu, and that's where I stayed the night."

I tried stopping myself from looking all the way to the left, but my eyes went there, and they locked with Brett's. God, he was like ice.

"We had sex at the hotel, and I got up the next morning and left. That's all that happened."

"And the video?" Jack asked. "Did Calvin tell you he was filming? Did you know you were being recorded?"

"No." My throat stung as I swallowed, feeling like a spotlight was shining directly above me and I was sitting on the stand. "I found out the same time everyone else did. Had I known I was being recorded, I obviously wouldn't have slept with him."

"Are you positive Calvin is the guy in the video?" Brett asked.

That was his first question, and it dug right into me.

"Yes."

He came back with, "How?"

I stared into those green eyes, my stomach churning, and said,

"Because I've slept with only three men. Abel, Calvin, and a man I was recently talking to until he broke things off."

I waited for the hardness to break, for him to show a little regret, sympathy—anything.

There was nothing.

"Has Calvin been located?" Scarlett asked.

I shook my head.

"Are the police looking for him?" Max asked.

"I haven't spoken to the police yet."

"What about the hotel?" Max asked. "Was the room in his name? Has your team questioned the hotel?"

I looked at Tim to answer, and he said, "No one has been questioned by her previous team. In my opinion, they checked out as soon as the video was released, and their resignations came as no surprise. There was a lack of planning and involvement, and all it's done is set James back because that time could have been spent fixing this damage." He turned his head, returning the stare, giving me the compassion I needed. "I think it's worth mentioning that James and Abel were represented by the same agent. I don't know if it was a conflict of interest, but once they broke up, I saw much less from him before he completely checked out."

When I turned toward the agents, they were glancing among themselves until Scarlett asked, "Have you been in touch with Calvin?"

"I never got his number."

"You never got his number?" Brett asked.

My stomach flipped again as my eyes traced back to his. "When I take someone's number, it's because I want to talk to them, and I make an effort to reach out. Calvin was a mistake, and he meant nothing to me. He still didn't when I woke up the morning after."

And, when I got back to LA, I would be throwing out the

handwritten number Brett had given me the morning after we slept together. I wasn't sure why I had kept it, as I should have tossed it days ago.

"There are pictures of you from last night. It looks like you were at a party, and you were dancing on a table," Max said.

Someone from the party must have taken those and shared them online. I was sure that was how my agent had known where I was when he called.

"In the media's eyes, it comes across as if you don't care that the video went viral," Brett said.

I don't care?

I shook my head, pulling Eve's jacket a little tighter around me.

I'd been completely professional up until this point, but to accuse me of not caring was where I drew the line.

"I'd been living in my closet since the alert went out. I hadn't eaten; I hadn't slept. I don't even remember leaving the room to pee." I glared at Brett, my voice getting much louder. "My whole world was crumbling, and the people who were supposed to be helping me had completely vanished. I don't even have my parents to turn to because they died three years ago in a car crash."

I looked to the right, away from him, away from that coldness. "Someone needed to throw my ass in the shower and make me feel like I had a reason to live. So, that's what my best friend did. She brought me to another friend's house where it was just supposed to be a few girls having a quiet night to help me get my mind off things. We had a couple of drinks and played some games. Then, the music turned on, and we wanted to dance. My best friend jumped on a table, and I joined her; it was completely innocent. But then a few people showed up and a few more, and then things got out of control. These strangers were calling me a slut and a whore. A guy put his hands all over me and..." I stopped to take a breath. "I had to hide in the fucking bathroom until Tim picked me up. Now, we're here." I lifted my foot, so they could see the slipper. "I didn't even have time to grab my shoes." As my slipper went back on the floor, I focused my gaze on Brett, my eyes not wavering one bit.

Finally, Max broke the silence with, "There's a lot of work that needs to be done. You have to speak to the police. The hotel needs to be questioned, and their security tapes have to be viewed. Calvin has to be found, and you need to formally press charges against him, assuming he's the one who set this up. It's an easy assumption, given that he blurred his face and masked his voice."

"What are you looking for, James?" Brett asked, and I stared at his lips as he spoke.

Emotion poured through my chest as I answered, "I've been working since I was thirteen years old to get to where I am." Those feelings moved up my throat and into my voice, and I did nothing to stop it. "Some asshole has taken that all away from me. I want it back. I want all of it back. And I want Calvin prosecuted, so the world knows I'm not the slut everyone is calling me."

I put my hand under my throat, trying to calm whatever was exploding in there. I watched Jack write something down on a piece of paper and slide it over to Brett. Brett read it, his jaw flexing as he bit down.

His eyes then moved to mine. "I need everyone to clear the room. James and I need to talk." When no one immediately got up, he growled, "All of you, out." He looked at Tim. "You, too."

Tim waited for me to give him a nod, a confirmation that I would be fine, and he got up from his chair and left.

I heard everyone else follow.

Now, it was just Brett and me, a giant table separating our chairs, and way too much silence.

13

BRETT

"YOU'RE SUCH AN ASSHOLE," James said, breaking the silence after everyone left the conference room.

She looked so tiny in that chair.

Tired.

Defeated.

And sexy as fuck.

"You've only seen my nice side," I told her. "You haven't seen my asshole side yet."

When I'd walked into the room and first spoken, I had seen the jolt that went through her body. Her back had gone straight, her hands grabbing those armrests like she was about to fall out of her goddamn seat. I had seen her heavy breathing, the emotion that filled her face when she finally looked at me.

I'd had a few minutes to prepare and get my shit in check.

Based on her reaction and what Tim had told us, James hadn't gotten that kind of warning.

"You kicked everyone out of the room, so what do you want, Brett?" she snapped.

I didn't like the anger in her eyes or the furrow between her brows.

Her face was too beautiful for that.

"Do you want to work with me, James?"

She laughed, and it sounded full of sarcasm. "I don't even know who the hell you are."

"That's not true."

She pushed her hands onto the table. "I thought you were an attorney." Her eyelids narrowed. "Why didn't you tell me your last name?"

"You never asked."

"I asked—"

"No, you asked me what I did, and I answered."

"That wasn't the correct answer. That was a fucking lie."

Her voice was becoming sharper. I didn't like it.

"I didn't lie," I growled. "I went to law school, I passed the bar in California and Florida, and my license is active. That makes me an attorney. I just don't practice law."

"You can spin it any way you want, Brett, but you're an agent, and you work in the industry. You should have told me." She pushed back in her seat with her arms crossed, covering those gorgeous tits. "And, the second that alert aired, you threw me away."

My jaw clenched.

She was right.

I hated to fucking admit it, but she was.

The whole time I'd been listening to her tell the story about the sex tape, I'd expected her to say it happened within the last month. Hearing that it was three months ago had been a surprise.

One that pleased me.

But one that still made me look like an asshole in her eyes.

"I thought you had filmed it recently."

"You thought..." And then her voice drifted off, as though she were processing what I had just said. "You thought I'd had sex with him while we were talking? You thought I'd cheated?"

"No."

"That's what it would be."

"We'd have to be together for that to happen. We weren't."

She shook her head. "Don't you get it? I wasn't talking to anyone else. It was just you. You were all I thought about. So, in my mind, that tied us together, and that's why it hurt so badly when you threw me away."

"Stop saying that."

"It's what you fucking did."

"James—"

"I know what it feels like to be cheated on. I wouldn't ever put anyone through that." She stood and walked over to the windows, pressing her hand on the glass. She stayed just like that for several seconds, looking at the view, and then she slowly turned around. There was even more anger in her eyes. "Did you fuck me that night just to get my business?"

My rage tripled hers.

I shoved myself away from the table, and by the time I reached her, she'd turned toward the windows again. My arms surrounded hers in a cage, my face dipping into her hair—the same way I had when we met, except I was behind her now.

"Get that out of your head," I barked, my teeth tight, my words commanding. "Every look you gave me at the bar, every word you said to me, every minute of silence that passed between us made my dick that much harder. I couldn't stop touching you, and I didn't want to. And I didn't want the night to end without my tongue licking your cunt. That's why I fucked you, James."

She didn't move, nor did she respond.

"Tell me what you want from me," I said.

"I want to know why you didn't text me back or answer my call. I want to know why I meant so little to you." There was so much pain in her voice. "I gave you my body, Brett. I held nothing back. And, every time we spoke on the phone, I told you so much about myself. I begged you to come to LA. I sent you pictures, hoping they would entice you to get on a plane. What else could I have done? Where did I fuck up?"

"Stop."

Both of her hands were now pushing into the glass. "There must be someone else because I really thought you wanted me. Or maybe you just realized I wasn't enough."

She sounded hurt. Pissed. Confused.

She had every right to be.

Moving quickly, not giving her a chance to react, I turned her around to face me, gripping her waist with all my strength. "Stop it, James, or I'm going to bend you over that table and spank your fucking ass until it's red."

"Had you picked up the phone, you could have been spanking me nights ago. Let me go. Now."

My teeth ground at the thought of that, and I pulled her body up against mine. "You were enough," I hissed, my lips moving to the side of her face.

She pushed my mouth off her and tried wiggling out of my grip. "Get away from me."

I grabbed her wrists and held them together. "James, listen to me, you were more than enough." I went in again, my lips now close to hers. "There was never anyone else. Only you. I couldn't get you off my mind. You need to believe that." I ground my cock into her stomach. "You make me so fucking hard." I twisted my hips, giving her my whole length. "Do you feel that? Do you feel what you do to me?"

Her body was still so rigid.

"Do you want an apology? Is that what you're looking for?" I breathed each word into her face. "Fine, I should have given you a chance to explain."

Her body relaxed a little.

"I fucked up." My nose grazed her cheek, and I took in a whiff of her pear scent. *Jesus, she smells so goddamn good.* "I'm sorry."

"You hurt me." Her voice was so soft.

"I know."

"You made me hate you."

I moved my lips to her collarbone and up her neck.

The moan she made was so fucking quiet.

I still heard it.

My mouth was making her feel good. So, I gave her more of it, kissing just to the side of her face and up the back of her ear. And, while I still held her with one hand, I moved the other down her chest. She stopped me when I reached the middle of her tits, her hands holding me still.

"I'm sorry," I whispered.

I took her earlobe into my mouth and gently sucked on it.

I missed the taste of her pussy, the way it had felt on my tongue. The sounds she'd made when I flicked across her clit.

Her grip began to loosen.

"Let go, James."

With her fingers still on mine, I moved my hand until it cupped her tit, my thumb gently brushing across her nipple. When her breathing increased, I rubbed harder, pinching it through the lace of her bra.

"Brett," she groaned, finally giving me the full sound I wanted to hear.

I turned her around and backed her up until the table hit her ass. Then, I reached around at the pile of notepads and pens resting on it, and I swiped them all to the floor. With both hands, I quickly unbuttoned, unzipped, and pulled down her jeans and panties until I had enough access to her pussy, and then I turned her once more, so she faced the table.

My hand froze as it touched my zipper. "I don't have a condom."

"It's okay." She then added, "I'm on something, and I'm clean; don't worry."

I turned her face toward mine, and the look in her eyes told me I could trust her. So, I released her cheek, and while I worked on pulling my cock out, I ran a finger up and down her cunt, making sure she was wet enough.

She was fucking dripping.

I wondered what had turned her on this much—if it was me telling her that I wanted to spank her or my apology or just the way I touched her.

With my dick now sticking out the hole of my boxer briefs and through my open zipper, I made her bend at the waist, pushing her upper body onto the table and holding her there. "James," I groaned as I slid in my crown. I hissed at the warmth that swallowed me, at the wetness that soaked me.

She felt unbelievable.

And she felt even tighter than the last time I'd been inside her.

I kept it slow for a few thrusts, waiting for her pussy to relax and get used to me again. Once I heard a deeper moan come through her lips, I knew she was starting to feel really good, and I held nothing back.

She could take it.

Every inch.

I kicked her legs further apart, continued to hold her flat, and rocked my hips to give her my full stroke. Pushing in harder, I arched my back, so I would hit the spot she liked.

The one that made her scream.

And, as she started to, I leaned over her back and said, "There are people out there who can hear us. Keep it down."

She whimpered, her arms extending over her head, her nails

trying to dig into the wood. "Oh my God," she said. "I'm going to come."

I could tell.

She was tightening around me. Pulsing. She even got a little wetter.

I put my hand on her pussy, holding her clit between two fingers, squeezing it with just enough tension, brushing the edge of it with my thumb.

"*Ahhh*," she breathed.

I knew every sound she made.

So, I knew she was holding herself back from shouting. I knew there was an orgasm ripping through her body. And I knew every wave she felt because she clenched me during each one.

I took the pressure off her back and grasped her hip, giving her more speed and power, fucking her as hard as I could.

"Brett," she cried out. "Don't stop."

I didn't need an order to stay buried in her pussy. It was the only place I wanted to be right now.

I reared back and sank in while grounding the pads of my fingers on her clit.

I could feel her getting ready to come again.

But so was I.

I shortened my strokes, rotating my hips, working the tingling sensation through my balls.

"Brett," she said again, her voice so raspy and sexy.

"Come right now," I demanded.

The last time I had been inside her, I'd had a condom on, the tight latex restricting the feeling. But here, I was uncovered, with the wetness of her pussy soaking me, the tightness milking the cum out of me.

One shot.

Then, a second.

"*Fuuuck*," I roared, trying to keep my voice down.

When I was empty, I slid my cock out and tucked it into my suit pants, zipping back up. I then reached for her jeans and pulled them up her legs until they cupped her ass.

She'd straightened off the table, but she still wasn't facing me.

She said nothing.

Neither did I.

My body just pressed against hers, feeling every breath, every exhale.

"Your cum just dripped out of me," she finally said.

I moaned as I thought about how fucking hot that would look. How I wanted to see my cum leaking out of her and onto a bed where I could watch the stain grow.

I lifted her hair off her neck and inhaled her skin as the scent was now mixed with mine.

"I don't have another pair of panties with me."

I moved to the other side of her throat, knowing the seconds we had together were limited. "I don't want you to change them. I want my cum dried on your pussy until you shower again."

After I said that, I knew I'd made another goddamn mistake. I never should have put my hands anywhere near her. Not when I wanted to work for her. Not when I knew she needed my expertise far more than she needed my cock.

"I've never done that with a client."

"Technically, I'm not one."

I couldn't say this into her back, so I quickly turned her around and held her. "Listen to me, you need my help, and I want to give it to you."

"Brett—"

I squeezed her hips, so she knew I wasn't playing. "I can make this better, James. My whole team can. We'll do everything it takes to get your career back. But I can't be fucking you at the same time."

Her eyes searched mine. "What are you saying?"

"I'm saying, this can't happen again."

"You're making me choose between you and professional you?"

I shook my head. "I'm telling you to sign with me."

Her eyes shifted between mine, the reality of my words finally starting to hit her.

"You want your career more than anything in this world," I said. "I'm going to get it back for you."

"But—"

I held her harder. "Trust me. I know what's best for you."

This was the last fucking thing I wanted, but I couldn't sleep with a client, not one who needed me this badly. She was going to have a few tough months ahead of her. Rumors of us dating wouldn't help her career. We had to kill the sex talk, not trigger more of it.

"What about what I want?" she asked.

"You're going to tell me what you want when I bring Tim and my partners back in and we finish this meeting."

It was a risk. James could out us in front of my whole team. But it was one I was willing to take.

"You're kidding," she said.

"That's why you're here, James. Don't let what just happened get in the way of what's important. Let me get back what you've lost and let me destroy Calvin Parker."

"Brett, I—"

I gently pressed my thumb against her lips, not letting her finish, and I sat her back in her chair. Then, I leaned down to kiss her forehead, keeping my face there for several seconds, breathing her in one last time.

As I headed to the door, I checked the front of my suit. Her wetness was on my tie, and there was more of it on my pants.

I closed the door behind me without saying another word and found the guys and Scarlett in her office. I stayed outside, only popping my head in. "I need to go to my office for a second, but I'll meet you back in the conference room in ten."

"Are you going to offer her representation?" Jack asked.

They were suspicious. I could tell by their expressions.

They had every right to be.

I'd never kicked any of them out of a meeting before.

"Yeah," I replied. "She's worth it."

14

JAMES

WHEN TIM CAME BACK into the conference room, I was sitting in the same place as when he'd left.

Seconds before he'd walked in, I had just finished picking up the notepads and pens that Brett had swiped onto the floor. As I'd squatted down to get them, more of his cum had dampened my panties. Fortunately, my tank top was long and covered the stains I was sure were soaking through.

I couldn't wrap my head around what we had just done.

But I knew my pussy was sore, my cheeks felt flushed, and my hair was probably even messier than before.

Brett had admitted he was wrong.

He'd apologized.

It was exactly what I'd needed from him.

And then the possibility of things between us going back to where they had been was completely taken away from me.

Brett had said that signing with him would increase my chance of getting my career back.

But that meant our relationship would only be professional.

His hands would never touch me again.

I'd never feel his skin against mine.

"Did the two of you work things out?" Tim asked with his eyebrow raised as he sat next to me. "I didn't realize you knew each other."

I turned toward him and opened my mouth, pausing as I thought about how I should respond. Tim had been with me since I was thirteen. He knew the details of what had gone on with Calvin; he certainly didn't need to know anything had happened with Brett. It wouldn't look good for either of us, especially since I'd already lost one agent.

"Things are fine now," I told him.

The door opened again, and the four partners walked in. Based on their expressions, I didn't think Max, Jack, or Scarlett knew that Brett had bent me over the table. But I wondered if they had noticed that Brett changed his suit. Instead of black, he now wore navy with a striped tie rather than a solid.

I wanted to ask him if we'd gotten something on it, but that wasn't really appropriate anymore.

"Here's how this is going to work," Brett said, sitting in the same seat he'd been in before. "I'm going to put together a contract that will outline my scope of work and the percentages I charge. If your attorney has questions, we'll address them. Once you're signed, my team will start working immediately."

"I just got off the phone with her attorney," Tim said. "He's aware of the situation, and he's promised to have the contract read by the end of the day."

"Good. Now, you're going to need a publicist. I have one on my team who's the best in the business. You're free to hire her, or you can look elsewhere, but you need someone to handle the media."

I glanced at Tim, and I could tell we agreed.

Tim's eyes moved from mine to Brett's, and he said, "We'll use yours to keep it all in-house."

Brett nodded and continued, "Assuming you sign the contract, you, Tim, and I will fly to LA tomorrow morning. My team will set up an appointment with the police, and you'll speak to them until they have all the information they need. Then, we'll swing by your house to get your personal items, and we'll fly right back."

"Wait." I glanced at Tim to see if that answer was on his face, too. He looked as clueless as me, which meant this was all news to him. "Why do I need to grab personal items?"

"Because you're moving."

I felt my eyes widen, and my hands gripped the edge of the table, pulling me closer to it. "I'm moving?"

"That's the only way this will work. I have to get you out of LA. It's toxic for you to be there right now."

"You want me in Miami?" I knew my questions were repetitive, but I couldn't believe what I was hearing. Moving here would only bring me closer to him, and that would make this even harder. "What do I get out of this?"

"You get the best fucking agent in the business." He took his jacket off and set it on the next chair, his cuff links banging on the wood as his arms returned to the table. "My plan is to reintroduce you to the media, but it has to happen slowly. We need to get them comfortable with you again. That means, keeping you out of the direct spotlight for just a little while. If we throw you right back in to auditions and industry parties in LA, you'll get rejected. That's why I'm scaling back, keeping you in Miami, starting with local fundraisers, charity events, places where you'll be noticed and photographed but in a positive environment."

He glanced down at his hands, and my eyes followed. My skin began to heat as I thought about the way he'd used them to hold me against the table and rub my clit.

"My team will decide what you wear. Whom you'll speak to."

His stare moved back to mine. "But something needs to be made extremely clear. I'm the boss. That's nonnegotiable."

"Where will I live?"

"Our realtor will find you a place," Scarlett said.

I'd almost forgotten Brett's other partners were still in the room with us.

"We'll have a lease signed before you return from LA. If the apartment isn't available for a few days, we have one here for our clients to use while they're in town. It's large enough for you and Tim, if you'd both like to stay there."

I knew Tim wouldn't be moving to Miami with me.

I didn't even know how I was going to move here.

Everything was spinning.

Fast.

And I had no control over any of it.

Brett's plan was going to change my whole life.

Again.

"You need to make a decision, James."

Everyone in the room was looking at me, waiting for an answer.

There were so many other agencies in LA and some in New York, and I hadn't met with any of them. I wondered what their ideas would sound like, if they would come up with a better plan than Brett's.

"You want your career more than anything in this world. I'm going to get it back for you. Trust me. I know what's best for you."

Brett's words repeated in my head.

Something made me want to trust him, to believe he would try his hardest to get back what I had lost.

Deep down, I knew he wanted me as badly as I wanted him. He just wanted to help me more.

I had to respect him for that.

Still, it stung like hell.

I glanced at the partners' faces, moving from Scarlett to Max and finally Jack. There was confidence in their eyes. Determination. A will that my old agent never had.

Then, I looked at Tim. I didn't need to ask what he wanted; I already knew.

My eyes shifted once more and fixed on Brett's.

I knew what this meant.

I knew what I would be giving up.

Somehow, I'd just have to find a way to accept it.

"Okay, let's do it," I told him. "Let's get me signed."

15

BRETT

I STOOD in the doorway of James's walk-in closet in her LA home, looking around the large room at each of the built-in racks and across the shoe and purse section in search of her suitcases. "Where are they?"

"All the way in the back," she said from the master bathroom as she packed up some of her shit. "They're on the left side, near my jackets, but on the very top where I can't reach." She paused, and I heard her feet on the hardwood floor. "Here, I'll show you." She moved past me and stopped once she stepped inside. "God, she cleaned everything up."

"Who?"

"My housekeeper." She crossed her arms over her chest, like she was hugging herself. "It was such a mess in here; there were clothes everywhere." Slowly, she turned toward me. "I told you I lived in my closet after the video was leaked. I wasn't kidding. I was too scared to walk by a window in case the paparazzi were in the trees outside."

Those fuckers were relentless.

I'd dealt with some who had done far worse than climb trees to get a photo.

She was staring at the space directly across from us, and I could tell she was remembering it all.

I didn't like the thought of her living in this room.

I didn't like what she had gone through.

I especially didn't like that she had experienced it alone, everyone but Tim leaving her.

Fuck, I should have handled shit differently.

"You all right?" I asked when she looked at me again.

Neither of us had moved. I wasn't even sure if she had taken a breath.

She nodded.

"You want to show me where the suitcases are?"

"Oh...*right.*" She walked toward the back left corner and pointed toward the ceiling. "They're up there."

I counted five. "You want me to take all of them down?"

"You said move, but does that mean permanently, or will I be in Miami for only a little while?"

"I don't know the answer to that yet, James."

She looked around her closet and said, "Just grab three. I can always have my housekeeper ship something if I need it."

I took down three of the suitcases and brought them to the center of the closet where I opened each one and spread it out over the floor. "Do you need me to reach anything else?"

She stood a few feet away, watching me. "No."

Tim had headed home once we were finished at the police station. He had young children and wasn't able to make the move, but he would come visit in the next week or so.

That meant we were alone in her house. In her bedroom. In a space that I wanted to throw her across the fucking mattress and bury my cock inside her.

"I'll wait for you in the kitchen," I said, taking out my phone as I walked there.

I responded to the inquires that concerned my clients, and then I called Scarlett. I wanted to update her on what had happened, so she could pass along the info to my team.

"How did it go?" she asked as she answered her cell.

"Not good." I opened the fridge, looking for a bottle of water and grabbed one when I found them in a drawer. "We were at the police station for almost the whole day. They couldn't find a Calvin Parker who fit James's description."

"I was afraid of that."

"Me, too." I moved over to the sliding glass doors and checked out her pool. "They're going to keep searching their database, but I don't think they're going to find him in there."

"If he blurred his face and disguised his voice, I'm going to bet Calvin Parker isn't his name."

"I'd double that bet."

"So, what now?"

I turned around, heading into her dining room on my way to the living room. "The police assigned her a sketch artist, and she and James worked on a drawing. But, Scarlett, it's been three months since she saw him. She was drinking that night and rushed out the next morning. I got the impression the details of his face were a little hazy, and James wasn't confident with what she had come up with."

"Has the hotel been questioned?"

"The police are going there tomorrow to request their security tapes." I took a long drink, finishing almost half of the bottle.

"Things are at least going in the right direction; that's good. How's she holding up?"

I looked around the corner at the door to her bedroom. She was still in there and had yet to bring out any of the suitcases. "The questioning at the police station got pretty intense, especially when she had to tell them what had happened at the hotel. She got all torn up and had to take a few breaks. She got through it; it was just really rough on her."

"And how are you doing with all this?"

"This isn't about me."

"Come on, Brett. Don't go and shut down on me now. I know you were hoping no one would notice, but when we got back to the conference room, it reeked of sex, and you changed your suit and tie. Maybe you fooled the guys, but you didn't fool me."

I sighed, shaking my fucking head.

Of course she had picked up on that.

"I'm not talking about this, Scarlett."

"You don't have to give me any details, but I need to know James can handle everything that's going on and focus on improving her image while balancing whatever is happening between the two of you."

"There's nothing happening," I growled.

"So, you're done?"

"Yes."

"Brett—"

"Scarlett, it's over," I hissed. "Next question."

She paused and then asked, "When are you and James coming back to Miami?"

"As soon as she's done packing."

"And Tim?"

"He's not moving, like we suspected."

I heard paperwork rustling in the background, and I took another sip.

"Should we look for a new manager?" she asked.

"I think he's good for her. Shit, he brought her to us. When she returns to LA, he can be more active. In the meantime, my team will do whatever she needs." I took a seat in front of the fireplace, which gave me a clear path to her bedroom door. "Did the realtor find James an apartment?"

Scarlett laughed. "Yes."

"Why don't I like the sound of that?"

"Because the apartment is in your building."

I rested my elbows on my knees and rubbed my forehead. "Jesus fucking Christ."

"The realtor asked if you'd have a problem with it. I didn't think you would. It's a big building, and you have your own private elevator that brings you straight to the penthouse. The chances of you running into her in the lobby or garage are slim to none. So, what's the big deal if she lives a few floors down?"

The big deal was that James was going to be in my office every day, and now, she was going to be in the building where I lived. There was no break. She would be everywhere I fucking turned, and I had to keep my hands off her.

"I can have the realtor keep looking, or I can forward you the lease for James to sign when you're on the plane."

My hand dropped from my forehead.

Scarlett was testing me.

"Send the lease," I said. "If James likes the photos, I'll have her sign it."

I moved over to the pictures that hung on the wall in the living room. There were at least thirty framed shots of James on different magazine covers and movie posters, and some were photos with her friends.

She was gorgeous in each one.

Just as gorgeous as the real thing, which was now standing outside her bedroom, all three suitcases in front of her.

Over the next few months, I'd be spending a lot of time staring at that face, thinking about it, exerting more restraint than I'd ever had in my life.

"When can she move in?" I asked.

"Tomorrow."

"Perfect. I'll see you in the morning." I hung up, and as I walked over to James, I said, "You got everything?"

"I think so."

"Then, let's go."

With a tumbler of scotch in my hand, one that had already been refilled twice during this flight, I opened my email and scrolled until I found the information the realtor had sent. It showed the layout of the apartment and multiple pictures of each room along with the terms of the lease.

I tilted my laptop toward James as she sat in the seat across from mine. "Here's the place that's up for rent."

She put her phone down and looked at the screen, checking out the pictures as I flipped through them.

"It's really nice," she said. As I got to the last shot, our stare met. "The view is pretty."

"It's available tomorrow. It's month to month, and it's close to the office. Or do you want the realtor to look for a different apartment?"

"No, it's fine."

Her eyes didn't convince me. Her voice was too soft.

"James, you need to be honest with me."

It was real fucking ironic I'd asked that of her when I couldn't be honest myself. Because, as much as I was listening and paying attention to what she wanted, I couldn't pretend like my thoughts weren't on her pussy. That the hard-on busting through my boxer briefs wasn't from staring at her lips and what I wanted her to do with them.

"All of this is just a lot," she said. "I had to hide from the paparazzi to get in and out of my house today. I'm all over the media, and people are saying the most horrible things about me. I'm moving..." She hesitated, chewing the inside of her lip, and it made my cock throb even harder. "And, now, you're my agent, and I'm supposed to pretend like nothing has happened between us and that you're not the guy I've been thinking about for the last month." She reached for her diet soda—a reminder she wasn't even old enough to order something stronger. "It's going to take me a minute to get used to everything."

She lifted her legs and bent them over the next seat, the yoga pants showing her long, lean thighs and the dip between them that housed that warm, tight cunt. The sweater that was supposed to be covering her tank top was open, revealing the curve of each tit.

I put my laptop in the bag and zipped it up, slamming the rest of the scotch. When I set the glass on the table, I checked the monitor that hung at the front of the plane. There was still four hours left of the flight. Staying in this seat, knowing she was this close, wasn't going to make this hard-on go away.

"Are you tired?" I asked her.

She shook her head. "But I'd like to watch a movie, if you don't mind."

I handed her the remote from the table and stood. "I'm going to head to the bedroom and try to get a few hours of sleep."

I didn't wait for her reply. I just turned around, adjusted my cock, and walked toward the back of the plane.

16

JAMES

Me: You're not going to believe this. Brett, the hottie from the bar, is an agent. MY new agent.
Eve: Shit like this only happens to you, I swear.
Me: He wants me in Miami for a while, thinks I need to get out of LA with everything going on. So, I'm on my way there now. In his company's private jet. With him. Alone. Gah.
Eve: I'm sick at the thought of you leaving me.
Me: Come visit. I'll buy you a ticket. When are you free?
Eve: I'll check my schedule and let you know. You'd better only be texting me because you and Brett are taking a break between rounds of him fucking the shit out of you. Give me details. I'm severely sex-deprived at the moment.
Me: He cut things off between us. He just wants to be my agent. That's it.
Eve: That's stupid. Is that what you want?
Me: I want him as my agent, AND I want him to be making me a member of the Mile-High Club right now. Sadly, that's not going to happen.

Eve: How do you know he won't change his mind? What's he doing right now?

BRETT HAD LEFT me to go into the bedroom about fifteen minutes ago. I'd tried searching for a movie, but I couldn't focus on what was on the screen. The thought of him in that bed was all that had been on my mind.

I needed to be close to him even if that meant just going to the bathroom.

So, I quietly got up and moved toward the back of the plane, wondering if he was on the phone or watching TV or if there would be silence in his room.

As I got closer, we hit a patch of rough air. The plane jolted, shaking beneath me, and I rushed to the side to hold on to a seat, so I wouldn't fall. It only lasted a few seconds, and then the turbulence was gone. But, in that time, it had been just enough movement for the door to crack open the tiniest bit and for light to seep out from the small slit.

Now, I had the perfect window to look through.

Tiptoeing, not wanting to make a sound, I positioned myself to the left of the door and quickly realized I was looking at his face. I shifted my stance, leaning more to the right, and this view was of his chest and stomach and—

I slapped my hand over my mouth to stop the noise that was about to come out.

Brett had his button-down shirt pushed up and his suit pants pulled down.

His hand was on his dick.

And he was stroking it.

God, it was the sexiest sight I'd ever seen.

I got closer to the opening to get a better view of his cock. I hadn't seen many in my life, but his was certainly the nicest. It was long and hard, a vein running down the backside and a thick crown circling the top.

The only sound that came from the room was his fist pumping.

And it was pumping so hard.

I wanted to wrap my mouth around the tip, taking him in my throat, my tongue swirling around his shaft as I pulled back, before I dipped in again, repeating that over and over until he came.

But Brett had made it clear that he only wanted me as his client. Nothing else, nothing that included my mouth or his cock. So, for now, all I could do was watch.

Wetness began to pool in my panties as his hand moved faster, deeper, gripping his dick like it was a baseball bat. He slid to the top and covered it with his palm before twisting as he went down about halfway and rose again.

The muscles in his thighs flexed.

So did those beautiful abs.

I knew I shouldn't be looking, but there was no way I could leave now.

Brett was getting close. I could tell because, both times I'd felt him come, he'd sped up right before he got off.

But, this time, I got to see the build, I got to see his fingers squeeze extra hard, and I got to see what pleasure looked like from his point of view.

And then I got to see him come.

Long ribbons of white shot out from the tip. I didn't know where it landed since that was outside my small window of viewing.

But I saw the way it projected and how his muscles contracted and his knees bent.

And I heard a noise that wasn't skin on skin. It was still quiet, surely because he didn't want the flight attendant or myself knowing what he was doing, but it was deep and guttural. And it was a moan, one he'd made every time he fucked me.

After the last stream of cum came out, his hand stopped, and I took a step back toward the bathroom, rounding the corner and rushing to my seat.

Several seconds passed. Then, I heard the door open and another one close, and I knew he had gone into the bathroom.

I wondered what had gotten him so hard. If he had hoped I wasn't tired and wouldn't take the bedroom from him, so he could go in there for some privacy. I wondered if the visual in his head had been of me.

I'd never get those answers, but my mind still came up with my own conclusion—one that involved Brett's desk, but this time, I was facing him, my legs spread across the edge, as he looked me in the eyes while he fucked me.

That thought was interrupted when my phone lit up on the table, and I saw Eve's name on the screen.

Eve: You totally just put the moves on him, didn't you?
Me: No! He's sleeping.
Eve: Go wake his ass up.
Me: Text me when you come up with a date. XO

I flipped through the movies and found one of my favorites, a love story between a maid and the president, and I wrapped myself up in my sweater.

There was a little less than four hours left of this flight, and I knew there was no way I could fall asleep now.

17

JAMES

EVE FLEW to Miami ten days after I moved into my new apartment. Now that my car had arrived from LA, I was able to pick her up from the airport. She practically tackled me as she climbed into the front seat. God, I'd missed her, and I hadn't realized how much until she was here. My filming schedule had kept us away from each other for months at a time, but I was usually so busy, I didn't notice how long I was gone.

That wasn't the case now.

Every day felt like an eternity.

I drove us to my building, and I brought her straight upstairs. She dropped her purse on the floor in the entryway, her suitcase right in front of it, and she walked over to the balcony. She stood in front of the glass, taking in the whole view, and then turned around to do a quick scan of the open space.

"Girl, this place is sick."

She was right, and it looked much nicer than it had in the pictures Brett showed me. Everything in here was so clean and sparkly and white—the floors, the walls, even the furniture. The pop of color came from the artwork and the view. The entire back wall of the apartment was all windows, and that was what you saw first when you walked in the door.

Some of the buildings across from mine were mirrored and shiny, and others were all white stucco, one even a light pink. Directly in the middle of the high-rises was a strip of ocean that was navy in the middle and teal where it neared the land.

It was nothing like LA.

But it was so beautiful.

"Isn't it?" I moved over to the couch where I spread across the whole corner and hung my legs over the side.

She sat next to me, sticking her feet in my lap, and said, "You still have no idea how long you're going to be here?"

"You know I have my first event coming up, so I think Brett's waiting to see how the media responds. If they boo me away from the camera, I'd say I'm going to be in Miami for a while."

"Oh, honey."

It had been a little over two weeks since the sex tape was leaked, and nothing had been resolved. The police still hadn't found Calvin. They had gone to the hotel in Malibu where we'd stayed, and neither of us appeared in any of the footage. They had no record of Calvin in their system, and the room we'd stayed in was supposedly vacant the night we were there.

All proof had completely vanished, and I didn't think that was a coincidence.

Calvin didn't want to be found, nor did he want to be blamed for the video, and he was doing everything in his power to make sure that didn't happen.

So, for now, until more evidence was found or brought forward, the case was at a standstill.

That killed me.

"Be honest with me," she said. "Are you hating it here?"

I thought about her question. "No. I just don't know anyone besides Brett, and it's not like he hangs out with me or anything.

My days consist of going to his office in the morning, doing the things he needs me to do, and then coming back here. I work out in the gym upstairs. I go to the pool. That's it."

The time I did spend with Brett wasn't exactly filled with warmth, and there really wasn't any small talk. We discussed plans and business and upcoming roles he thought I would be good for, but the timing to try out wasn't right.

He was distant but professional—a side of him I respected. I just wished he would give me more.

Of course, more would mean crossing a boundary, and I knew he didn't want that.

"You do have a killer tan." She held her arm next to mine, and my skin was several shades darker than hers. "It's sorta like you're on vacation."

"One I wish I had chosen and not been forced to take."

She propped her arm on the back of the couch and rested her cheek against her palm. "You're in Florida. It's hot and sunny, and there are sexy people everywhere. I would say there are much worse gigs than this."

She was trying to be positive where I was so negative.

But she had a point. This break gave me some time to relax, something I hadn't done much of in the last year. It gave me a chance to watch lots of movies and read and workout. It allowed me to get settled in my new apartment.

And it gave me time to think about what I really wanted, which was to be on a movie set. I knew that now more than ever.

"Show me the schedule Brett's team put together for you."

I took out my phone and looked through my emails until I found the one that detailed the next several weeks. Each event was broken down by date with a full description of what the event was for, the dress code, the location, sponsors, and any high-profile people who would be attending.

"So, you have a gala along with several cocktail parties. Four charity events and a polo match." She glanced up. "Polo?"

I shrugged. "I guess it's a thing here."

"Okay…" She paused but kept her eyes on me. "You know, there is something extremely erotic about men riding horses while holding long sticks."

I laughed.

"The real Debbie Downer is that we have to make you look appropriate, which means pastels and capris and a sweater tied around your shoulders."

"Sounds like something Brett would approve of."

She rolled her eyes. "My goal is to have Brett approve everything." She pointed at the screen and counted each of the events. "I'd say ten to twelve dresses—a few of those formal—a light-pink paisley ensemble, and some casual outfits will get you by for now. If you need more, that will give me an excuse to come visit sooner."

Eve had been my stylist for years. When it came to clothes, I trusted her more than anyone. That was why, after we'd returned to Miami from LA, I'd begged Brett and his team to let her dress me for the events. They had requested a phone interview and for Eve to submit her portfolio, and she'd done both. Just yesterday, they'd given her their approval, but under one stipulation—they wanted her in Miami to get started immediately.

She was here less than twenty-four hours later.

"Do you have to leave to go shopping?"

She had a surprised look on her face. "Leave you? Oh no. I pulled clothes in LA, and they'll be here tomorrow morning. There are a few more things I need, so I'm going to call my assistant and have her ship them overnight. Now, there's just one more thing I have to take care of."

She took out her phone and tapped the screen, holding it to her ear. "Hi, Rachel. It's Eve Kennedy. I'm in town. I have a client who's attending a polo match in a few weeks, and I think several pieces from your new line would be perfect." She paused. "Yes, I would love that." She put her hand over the speaker and whispered, "What's the name of this building?"

"The Jewel," I said softly.

"Please have them delivered to The Jewel, attention to Eve in unit ten-fourteen." She paused again. "I'll have my assistant follow up with payment information and sizes. Thank you." She set her phone down. "Polo gear will be here tomorrow, and while we're at the pool, I'll call my assistant to coordinate the rest."

"I seriously love you."

"This is why we need to get your ass back to LA because living there without you is all kinds of wrong." She got up from the couch and grabbed my hand, pulling me off and leading me toward the bedroom. "We need bikinis and cocktails. Right now."

18

BRETT

I TOOK the private elevator down to the lobby of my building to pick up the pizzas Max and I had ordered. He'd been traveling for the last week, and this was the first time we had a chance to hang out, so he wanted to do dinner and watch the Heat game at my place.

As I went around the corner of mailboxes and past the doorman's desk, I saw James walking into the building.

Fuck.

She was only a few feet from me, and my eyes took in her small black bikini and the see-through cover-up she was wearing over it. I wished I hadn't because, the second my stare landed on that tight, perfect body, my dick started to harden in my sweats. My hands twitched to touch her. My mouth watered to taste that delicious cunt.

"Brett?" she said, halting in front of me—a spot I'd hoped she'd avoid and go straight to the elevator instead. "What are you doing here? Were we supposed to meet or something?"

Scarlett had said the chances of us running into each other would be slim.

She couldn't have been more fucking wrong.

"That's Brett?" the girl standing next to her said. "As in, *the* Brett?"

The girls looked at each other, and James's eyes widened, as though she were trying to silently say something to her.

Jesus Christ.

I turned toward the girl and extended my hand, knowing it was James's stylist who had flown in from LA. She had on almost the same bathing suit as James and looked great in it but not as good as James. And, even though she was really attractive, she wasn't as beautiful.

"Nice to meet you."

"You, too. I'm Eve."

Behind the girls, I saw the doorman take the pizza boxes from the delivery driver, and he came over to hand them to me in exchange for the fifty I had taken out of my pocket.

"Why are you getting food delivered to my building?" James asked as my attention returned to her.

"It's my building, too."

Her eyes widened even more. "You're kidding."

"No."

"Why didn't you tell me you lived here?"

I reached inside the box, grabbing a slice of pepperoni, took a bite of the end, and swallowed. "Would it have changed your mind?"

She opened her mouth, but nothing came out of it.

As though Eve were reading her, she cleared her throat and said, "I have all of James's outfits planned for her upcoming events. Why don't you come over, so you can approve or nix the dresses?"

"Eve," James said, hitting her friend's arm, "I'm sure Brett's too busy to come over."

If that meant seeing some sexy dresses on the body I'd been thinking about nonstop, then I wasn't too busy.

"Nah, I think that's a good idea." I took another bite. "I've got Max upstairs. I'll grab him, and we'll come down to your place."

"Who's Max?"

"One of the other agents," James said to Eve. Then, she asked me, "Are you really coming over?"

I nodded. "You hungry, or should we eat before we come?"

"We're hungry," Eve answered.

James looked at Eve again. "I guess we're hungry."

I could tell James still hadn't gotten over the shock that we lived in the same building. Hell, I hadn't gotten over how fucking perfect she looked in that bikini.

But it seemed she wore that expression almost every time I was around her—whether it was in my office or when I'd rejoined her on the plane after my long nap.

She was struggling with the transition.

I was, too.

I'd been rubbing one out almost every morning in the shower and again when I got home from work. Sometimes, when she came in for a meeting, I'd even do it in the bathroom in my office after she left. And I would once more tonight after I saw her in those dresses.

"I'll be at your place in a little while," I told them.

Then, I headed toward my elevator, waving the fob in front of the reader and pressing the PH button as I got inside.

When I stepped into my condo, Max was on the couch, watching the Heat game.

"Get up. We're going to James's."

In the kitchen, I grabbed a twelve-pack, knowing she probably didn't have any beer at her place, and carried it into the living room. The motherfucker still hadn't stood, but he'd turned off the TV, and he was staring at me.

"What?"

"Why the fuck are we going to James's?"

"I just saw her downstairs with her stylist, and they need my approval on some outfits."

"And what am I? A chaperone?"

I didn't want to tell Max I had been doing everything I could to keep my hands off James and that having him there would ensure I didn't touch her.

"You're the fourth wheel."

"Not interested."

"Her stylist is hot as fuck. Trust me, brother."

"Now, I'm interested." He got up and took the boxes out of my hand. "It surprises me that you let the realtor move James into your building."

"Why?"

"You won't even bring the women you fuck back to your place because you don't want them to know where you live, but you'll let James be a neighbor."

"It's different."

He smiled and laughed as we walked into the elevator, and I hit the button for James's floor.

"What's so funny?"

"Something tells me you didn't mind running into her."

"Jesus, don't start with me."

First, Scarlett, and now, Max. The only one left was Jack, and I was sure he would have said something similar if he were here and not on the road with one of his clients.

Max kept laughing and shook his head. "I'm not starting shit. I'm just saying, if a girl who looked like James lived in my building, I wouldn't exactly be pissed off about it. But you're not me, and going down to her apartment isn't you."

"She's my client."

"So, that makes this different? If anything, it should make it worse."

"It makes her off-limits." I'd been facing the door, but now, I turned toward him. "We're going to her place to see some dresses. That's it."

"Something you could do in the office."

"You're fucking starting again."

"And, now, I'm dropping it."

I glanced away, not wanting him to see my eyes, and waited for the door to open. Since James had an end unit that faced the water, I headed east when I stepped out and knocked on the last door.

Eve answered, holding it open enough for us to walk in.

I went in first and heard Max introduce himself to her as I made my way toward the kitchen, grabbing a beer before putting the case in the fridge.

"James will be right out," Eve said. "She wanted to take a quick shower before she tried anything on."

I wished she hadn't told me that. The thought of James in the shower, her body wet and covered in bubbles, made my cock hard.

Eve took a slice of pizza and sat on one of the ottomans while Max and I took spots on the other side of the couch.

"I spoke to your team and kept their recommendations in mind when choosing each dress," she said. "Several are black, but more than half are in jewel tones, which look incredible with James's skin tone. I understand the need to keep her in conservative pieces, leaning more toward mature than youthful, but I don't want her dressed like a fifty-year-old either. There's a balance, and we'll find it."

Max wedged his beer between his knees and started on his first slice. "When does the fashion show start?"

"Right now," James said.

The three of us turned in her direction.

Holy fuck.

The dress she had on was a deep red, and it hit just above her knees, wrapping around her whole body up to her chest, leaving her arms exposed. It would keep the media quiet by covering what it needed to, but it was sexy and mature, making her look far older than eighteen.

This was how we would earn back the public's respect.

Because this was how a woman dressed when she wanted to be taken seriously.

And, goddamn it, it looked gorgeous on her.

"This is what I call cocktail attire, and it would be perfect for one of the charity events," Eve said. "She'll pair the dress with the four-inch heels she has on, a black clutch, diamond jewelry, and I recommend she wear her hair up. Her shoulders are too beautiful to cover."

James grabbed the wet hair that hung around her face and held it on top of her head.

I didn't know how, but it made her look even hotter.

"Turn around, James," Eve said.

The dress hugged her ass and the curve of her hips, and although it didn't show what was underneath, in my head, I saw where her thighs met and the tight little cunt that sat between.

Feeling Max's eyes on me, I looked away and walked over to the table to grab another slice of pizza.

"So, what do you think?" Eve asked.

I faced James again and said, "It's good. Let's see the next one."

James disappeared down the hallway, and I went back to the couch.

"How many will she be trying on?" I asked.

"Twelve."

Jesus, fuck.

I had to go through this eleven more times.

Max reclined into the couch, kicking his legs onto the ottoman. "Looks like we're going to be here for a while, so I might as well get comfortable."

If my cock wasn't so goddamn hard, I would have done the same. But leaning back in these sweatpants would show everyone in this room what that fucking girl did to me.

James sat several cushions down, finishing her third slice of pepperoni. For someone so little, she could put down a hell of a lot of food.

I liked that about her.

And I liked seeing the grease on her fingers and a little more on her mouth and that she didn't wipe her face after every bite. I didn't want perfect, and James wasn't trying to be.

"She's a huge music fan," James said, referring to Eve, who was standing on the balcony with Max. "She's going to drill him until he can't take another question."

"He loves it, I'm sure."

He did, too. I could tell by the way he was looking at her as she spoke.

Eve was his type. A little wild, extremely mouthy, and aggressive as hell.

She was the opposite of James.

"You didn't say much about the dresses besides giving us your approval." She turned her face toward me, pressing her cheek into the back of the couch. "I know they're appropriate and all, but do you think they'll be okay? I want the media to see me differently now. I'm not a kid. But I'm not the names they're calling me either. I'm somewhere in the middle...in a very strange place."

The last time I'd heard this tone was on the plane.

Then, I hadn't been able to give her the attention she needed. My cock had been too fucking hard, and I'd had to get away from her before I tried to fuck her again.

She'd been hurting.

She was hurting now again, too.

The sex tape had stripped her self-confidence. She needed to be reassured, and she was looking to get that from me.

But I had to be careful.

"Don't stress about them." I slammed back the rest of my beer, knowing there was more in the fridge, but I didn't want to leave her just yet. "You looked great in all of them."

"Really?"

There was so much more I wanted to say, so many things that would put the biggest fucking smile on her face. But I couldn't tease her like that. That was what Eve was for. She'd tell James how stunning she looked and how the dresses perfectly fit her body and how she would be the hottest woman at every event.

And, as for me, I had to get some sleep.

I had a meeting in the morning, and I had to fly to Alabama in the afternoon to visit a client on set. The director was a good friend of mine. He'd sent me his next three screenplays, asking if I had anyone to fill the lead roles. James would be perfect for one. He owed me a favor, and I was going to cash in when the time was right.

With her face still pointed at me, I saw the emotion in her eyes. I saw the hunger. The desire. And, so fucking badly, I wanted to reach forward and pull her toward me, so her lips pressed against mine.

But I couldn't.

"I'll see you at the office in the morning." I went over to the glass door and opened it. "I'm going to head up," I said to Max.

"I'll be there in a little while," he said.

I slid the door closed and walked past James on my way out, feeling her eyes following me.

"Brett," she said as my fingers wrapped around the handle.

I turned around.

"Thanks for coming over."

Her voice was so soft.

I nodded and went to the elevator, knowing, the second I got upstairs, I would head straight for my shower where I'd wrap my fist around my fucking cock.

19

BRETT

I ARRIVED at the gala before the rest of my team, so I could get a few cocktails down and meet with the executives who were putting on the event. They were all affluent members of Miami society, and I wanted James to be seen with them and photographed with their wives. It wouldn't just look good for her image, but there was also a chance it could help her career since several of the men were retired from the industry.

Miami was where old Hollywood money came to retire and die, and these men were part of that generation. At times, the ones who didn't participate in the everyday hustle had more pull than the guys who worked it full-time.

I needed their connections.

So, I sat with the old-timers, sipping my second tumbler of scotch, and listened to them talk about property tax and the Dolphins and how to convert a chlorine pool to fucking saltwater.

I was putting in my time.

And it was noticed.

Henry, a movie producer who had been in the business for over forty years with a stack of awards that was highly impressive, asked me to follow him to get a drink. Adjusting the tie of my tux, I walked behind him and leaned into the bar top as he took a seat beside me.

"What would you like?" Henry asked me as the bartender stood in front of us.

"Whatever he's having"—I pointed at Henry—"I'll take the same."

As Henry ordered, I felt my phone vibrate from my inside pocket and quickly checked the screen. It was a text from Scarlett, saying she was on her way with Max and Jack and James was in a separate limo with a few of my team members. I stuck it back in my pocket and lifted the glass from the countertop, clinking it against Henry's.

"I hear you have a new client," he said. He ran his hand over his beard, one that looked like it hadn't been trimmed in months. "She's got some talent, that girl."

"She does."

"I hope you're helping her navigate all the trouble she's found herself in."

I nodded. "We're working with the authorities. It hasn't been as easy as we all would like, but some evidence will surface soon. I'm confident of that."

"Vaults are only as strong as their key holder. If I've learned anything from this industry, it's that those holders have a weakness. You just have to find it."

"I will."

"I don't doubt that." He took a drink. "What can I do to help you, Mr. Young?"

My trip to Alabama had been successful. The client I'd visited was made for the role, and I was sure the Academy would take note. The other half of the trip, I'd spent talking to the director about the movie he was going to be filming early next year and the lead that hadn't yet been casted. It was a drama that would be shot in Alaska where a young fisherman and his wife were in the Bering Sea, and fifty miles from shore, their boat would capsize and sink. It was a hell of a script, and James would be perfect for the wife. As long as the media calmed down, the role would be hers.

I would make sure that happened.

But it still wasn't the blockbuster I was looking for.

That was where Henry came in.

"James has lost all of her upcoming films. One of them is anticipated to be the biggest movie next year, and it's a role she's worked her entire career to land."

He pushed his glasses up and nodded. "I heard."

"I need to get her another one just like it."

"I had a feeling." He turned toward the bar and took several sips of his drink. "Let me put out some feelers and see what's in the pipeline."

"That's all I'm asking." I placed my hand on his shoulder. "I know you and your wife are Knicks fans. They'll be playing the Celtics in a few weeks, and I'd like to send you both to Manhattan for the weekend. Floor seats, full access to my company's private jet."

"Sounds like something my wife and I would like very much."

I squeezed his shoulder and made it about ten feet before I was approached by Rebecca, one of my clients.

She kissed me on the cheek and hugged me, and as I pulled away, she grabbed my hand and said, "Brett, I just saw him."

"I assume you're talking about the CEO of Netflix, and before you ask, he's already looking forward to meeting you. I'm going to take you over to him in about ten minutes."

"This is why you're the best."

Rebecca was one of my leading actresses, who dabbled in writing and directing. She had recently finished scripting her first series, and I wanted to pitch it to Netflix. It would be a huge hit for direct streaming, and I had high hopes they would bite. Given that the CEO was attending tonight's gala, I thought this was where we should start.

What Rebecca didn't know was that HBO was also here, and we would be meeting with them right after.

I could tell she was nervous, so I'd keep the second pitch in my back pocket until she made it through the first.

"Did you review the notes I sent you?"

Because I had known she'd be anxious, I'd had my team put together some talking points that would keep her on subject. The setting was informal, and she wasn't expected to be perfect, but this was an imperative step. If the CEO showed interest, the process would move quickly, and within a few days, we could be at their headquarters in Los Gatos.

She needed to be ready for that, and my team would prep her.

"Yes," she said, a smile covering her whole face. "Each point has been memorized." She gripped my hand harder. "You're so good to me."

As I started to reply, I saw James in the corner of my eye, and I turned my head just enough to see the rest of her. She stood near the entrance with several of my team members, wearing my favorite dress out of all the ones Eve had chosen. It was black and floor-length, wrapping around her neck and down her arms with cutouts on both shoulders and hips. It revealed just enough skin to make it incredibly sexy, and it hugged her flawless body.

My team would keep her busy for the next hour, introducing her to the wives of the executives and the other attendees we'd targeted when we got a copy of the guest list. Once Rebecca and I finished with both networks, James would get my full attention.

There was a vibration in my inside pocket, and I pulled out my phone to check the screen. It was another text from Scarlett, saying the red carpet had gone extremely well, the photographers had played nice, and no one had given James a hard time.

That was the way I'd planned it.

And that was what I'd fucking paid for.

This morning, cash had been wired to the photographers' accounts with an order to release the shots to all major celebrity sites before the gala was over.

This was James's first media appearance since the video had been leaked. So, I wanted the public to see how amazing she looked and how professional she was on the red carpet despite the things that had been said about her. I wanted it to be known that the gala was for charity and that James had made a sizable donation.

She wasn't going to hide anymore, but each sighting was going to be planned. And, each time, she would look hot as fuck and sophisticated, just like she did right now.

Tonight would be one of the best evenings she'd had since the tape was aired.

I'd make sure of that.

"How much time do we have until the meeting?" Rebecca asked.

Her hand was on my shoulder, and she was fixing the strap to her shoe.

"About eight minutes." I looked for James but no longer saw her near the entrance, which meant my team was taking her to her first introduction. "I'm going to grab you a drink, and I'll meet you over there in five." I pointed at the archway that was between the ballroom and bar.

"Make it a stiff one."

As we parted, I headed to the same spot where I'd talked with Henry, and just as I placed both drink orders, Jack joined me.

"She did good," he said, taking one of the drink straws out of the holder and chewing on the end. "But I'm sure Scarlett told you."

"Yeah, she texted me."

The bartender handed me two scotches, and Jack ordered one as well.

"It's going to be a busy night," he said. "I have six clients here and two prospective ones. And do you see those two women over there?"

I looked to where he was nodding, and there were two chicks standing near the corner of the room. One appeared to be in her fifties and the other in her twenties.

"Don't even fucking tell me."

He laughed, taking the drink from the bartender and holding it up to his lips. "I didn't know they were mother and daughter. Fuck, I didn't even know they knew each other."

"Which one do you like more?"

He glanced at them and then at me. "Do I have to choose?"

I laughed even harder than him and finally said, "We've got some good meetings tonight that could earn The Agency a shit-ton of money."

"Then, don't fuck them up. The last thing we need is you covered in cum."

My brows rose. "What?"

"I saw your tie when you came out of the conference room with James. Then, when we went back in to meet with her, the whole fucking room reeked of sex."

"Jesus Christ."

It was Jack's turn to dig, so I wasn't surprised I was getting that from him. I was just surprised it had taken him this long to bring it up. I was sure he'd been holding it in, waiting for the right time to lay it on me.

He clinked his glass against mine even though we'd both taken several sips. "You still tapping that?"

I shook my head.

"Are you fucking crazy? Why not? Do you see what she's wearing tonight?"

"She looks good; I know."

"Then, what's the issue?"

"She's eighteen years old, Jack." That didn't seem to dent his opinion, so I added, "She deserves a guy who is good at committing and isn't a serial bachelor." That didn't do anything either. "She's my client, and this isn't the right time to start anything. James needs to chill out for a while. Getting involved with me won't help her situation at all."

"I still don't know why you stopped tapping that."

"I need her to focus. I need to fucking focus. I can't do that if every meeting gets cut short because my dick has more to say than I do."

"So, have the meeting, finish what you need to say, and then dip it in."

"You're not helping."

"Trust me, my friend, I'm fucking helping you plenty. Any guy in this room would give you the same advice."

I looked at my watch and saw I had a minute left before I needed to meet Rebecca. "I've got to go pitch Netflix. I'll catch you later."

"Attaboy; go get that money," he said.

And I walked away.

20

JAMES

TONIGHT'S GALA was going exactly the way I'd hoped. The dress I wore was so perfect, my hair and makeup hadn't looked this good since my last movie premiere months ago, and no one had said anything negative to me yet, not even the photographers I'd posed in front of on the red carpet.

But I had been here for almost three hours, and Brett hadn't spoken to me once. However, he'd spent time with every other person in this room, especially the women he'd talked to at least twice. And then there was the one he was chatting with now. Her name was Rebecca Andrews—an actress I'd never worked with, but I'd heard lots about. I also knew she was single, and she'd been flirting with Brett every chance she got. Now, her hand was on his chest, her lips pulled in a smile, her eyes wide and gleaming, like she wanted to eat him in that handsome tux and that deliciously short beard he was now sporting.

I knew the feeling.

Every time I saw him, he made me feel the same way.

But Brett wouldn't let my mouth anywhere near him. Instead, he had his team doing all the work, where they told me to plaster a permanent grin on my face while they introduced me around the room. Their hope was that, after people had a conversation with me, they wouldn't look at me like I was a porn star, but an actress who valued my career and was passionate about the industry.

It was working.

During all my schmoozing, I'd been invited to lunches, garden parties, and more charity events, and a group of women had even invited me for tea. Brett's team was keeping track of the requests and would follow up to schedule dates, so I could focus on keeping my smile and giving the right answers.

I appreciated the acceptance I had been getting from the crowd. That was what I wanted after all.

I just wished Brett's attention could be included. That, for my first event, he could make me feel as though I mattered, that I was as important as all the other women in here.

To make matters even worse, I'd received a celebrity alert about an hour ago that said Abel and Sophia had gotten engaged in Fiji.

Fiji had been our place.

Apparently, it was now their place, too.

As I glanced to my left, I saw Rebecca's hand had lowered to Brett's forearm, and she was rubbing it back and forth. He was doing nothing to stop her. In fact, the expression on his face was only encouraging her to do it more. If those were my fingers, he would have removed them.

I wondered what made her different.

Maybe he hadn't slept with her and respected her more than me.

I'd learned, during my time in Florida, that Brett was named Miami's most eligible bachelor and was on the front cover of *Miami Magazine*. He was certainly living up to his name.

I faced the other direction, unable to look at them anymore, and saw Max approaching our small group.

"How's everything going?" he asked.

Jack and Scarlett had come over throughout the night to check on me, so I'd expected Max to be next, especially because he'd slept with Eve. The two of them had gotten it on in my guest room the night they met, and they'd been talking every day since she flew back to LA. This morning, she'd texted me that she was planning another trip here to visit us both.

"It's going pretty great," I replied. "I've made some strong connections, and everyone has been really nice."

"That's what I like to hear. Do you need anything?"

I shook my head. "Brett's team is taking good care of me."

"Where is that motherfucker anyway?" He looked to the side of us, spotting Brett less than ten feet away. "Ah, he's talking to Rebecca."

Her hand was still on his forearm, her thumb caressing the sleeve of his jacket.

"Did you get a chance to meet the head of the hospital?" he asked me. "I'm not sure if he and his wife were on your list, but you'll be seeing them at lots of other events, and it would be good if you knew each other."

"They were introduced already," one of the team members said, "and his wife asked James out for lunch."

"Looks like you're ahead of me," Max answered, laughing.

I didn't know why, but I turned to my left again and saw Rebecca whispering in Brett's ear.

I couldn't watch this shit anymore.

"Do you mind if I take a quick trip to the ladies' room?" I asked.

I didn't know whom I was asking but felt I needed to say something before I just walked away.

I felt Max's stare on me, but he wasn't the one to respond.

That came from another one of the team members, who said, "No problem. We'll wait for you right here."

Heading in the opposite direction from where Brett stood, I made my way outside the ballroom and followed the signs to a hallway and through a door that was across from the men's room.

I didn't look at any of the women standing around the sink. I just went right into a stall and locked it. Not needing to go to the bathroom, I leaned against the metal wall and took out my phone to text Eve, seeing that she had already sent me one.

> Eve: *Fuck Abel and Sophia. Those two miserable assholes deserve each other.*
> Me: *I haven't thought much about it. But Fiji? Really? I mean, at least he was creative with me.*
> Eve: *He's a dick. We know this. How's the gala? You look SO hot in the pic you sent.*
> Me: *It's been a little overwhelming at times, but everyone has been really pleasant. Thank God. Max is here in a tux, looking so dapper.*
> Eve: *I know. We video-chatted before he left, and I about died when I saw him. How's the other sexy agent?*
> Me: *I don't know. He hasn't said a word to me.*
> Eve: *Another dick.*
> Me: *Whatever. But, as his client, I thought he would at least say something. And, as someone who has slept with him, I just expected a lot more.*
> Eve: *I haven't brought it up to Max.*

My heart sped up as I read her words.

She'd promised she wouldn't say anything to Max about Brett and me. The last thing I needed was Brett hearing that I had been talking to my friends about what had happened between us. Eve had thought that, by saying something to Max, she could dig a little and find out how Brett really felt about me.

I had immediately shot that down.

> Me: *Good, because then I would have had to kill you.*
> Eve: *Who would dress you then and constantly make you laugh with inappropriate humor?*
> Me: *I'd miss you terribly; it's true.*
> Eve: *If Brett doesn't say something to you soon, I'm going to get extremely stabby.*
> Me: *I'll text you when I get home.*
> Eve: *If I don't respond right away, it's because I'm having wild phone sex.*
> Me: *I can't even with you.*
> Eve: *That's why you love me.*

I put my phone back in my clutch, flushed the empty toilet, and went out to wash my hands. While I squirted soap into my palm, I overheard the conversation happening two sinks down. I didn't recognize the women, but from what they were saying, I could tell they were talking about Rebecca Andrews.

"She's not single," one of them said. "I've seen her all around town with Brett Young."

"Maybe they just work together?" the other one asked.

"Possibly, but did you see the way she's been acting tonight? You'd think she was just attending, so she could make their relationship public."

"She does seem extra giddy."

"Giddy? That's because he probably took her into his limo and screwed her brains out."

"I did see them leave the ballroom together. Oh my God, this is so juicy. I can't wait to tell the girls at lunch tomorrow."

I wanted to throw up.

Brett had disappeared for a while. Not once, but twice.

And I knew how he liked to fuck people in public places where he could easily be caught, like a conference room...or the back of his limo.

I quickly dried my hands and slipped out before the women looked in my direction, and just as I was walking into the ballroom, Anthony Dine, the quarterback for Miami, said, "Hey." He looked at both sides of me. "Where's your entourage?"

I laughed.

Anthony and I had already met tonight when Brett's team introduced us.

"They took off the handcuffs, so I could use the ladies' room."

"Isn't that nice of them?" He glanced at my fingers, and then our eyes connected again. "You're empty-handed. How about we get you a drink?"

Anthony was even taller than Brett and had a completely different look to him with shaggy blond hair, deep blue eyes, and a smile that made you want to grin in return.

"I'd like that."

He stuck his arm out, and I looped mine through it before we walked to the closest bar.

"Vodka tonic," he said to the bartender.

She looked at me.

"Just a Diet Coke, please."

"That's all you want, big spender?"

I felt my cheeks blush.

Before the tape had been leaked, I would have ordered a cocktail. But, now, I just wanted to be extra careful about every move I made, and drinking in front of all these people didn't feel like a smart one.

"I'm not really a drinker," I lied.

"Nothing wrong with that." He grabbed my soda and gave it to me. Then, he slid his hand into his pocket and pulled out some cash that he dropped into the tip jar. "How long are you in town for?"

He took his drink, and we stepped away from the bar and moved toward the side of the room where it was a little quieter.

"I'm not sure," I said. "Probably several months at least."

"Are you filming?"

He obviously wasn't a subscriber of celebrity alerts because several had gone out following the sex tape that notified the world that I'd lost my upcoming movie deals and that I was unemployable. Or maybe he had seen them and was acting dumb.

"Not at the moment."

"So, what are you doing in Miami?"

I wasn't sure how to answer his question, so I said, "I'm just taking some time off. Focusing on me. It's been a while since I've done that."

"Looks like you're focusing on your tan, too. Damn, girl, you're darker than me during football season."

I smiled. "I like the pool."

"The pool? You're in Miami. Why aren't you going to South Beach? That's where you and your little bikini should be going every day."

I laughed at the expression on his face, and just as my head straightened, he reached forward and moved a piece of hair off my lip. It caught me off guard, and I heard myself suck in a breath. He must have heard it, too, because he chuckled a little, and I swore, he took a step closer.

"A few of us are going back to my place after this. You should come. It'll be fun."

I suddenly felt a hand on my lower back, and my nose filled with Brett's spicy scent. Just as I turned, I met his face. But he wasn't looking at me; he was staring at Anthony.

"Anthony," he said, "I've got to steal James for a second."

"Bring her right back," Anthony replied.

Brett laughed, and I felt the push of his palm to get me to start walking. "Smile," he whispered in my ear. "People are watching."

I did as he'd told me, dropping the scowl that had been there previously, and I followed him around the side of the ballroom and out the back where an SUV was parked right by the door.

"Get in," he ordered.

"What? Why?"

"Because tonight is over."

"For what reason?"

"You've spent enough time here, and you met the people I needed you to. Now, you're going home."

"Are you punishing me?"

"Get in," he growled.

"Brett, you're acting ridiculous." And then it hit me. "Are you mad that I was talking to Anthony?"

"I'm not having this conversation out here." He opened the back door, moving me over to it and urging me inside. He got in behind me and said to the driver, "Go ahead and take us to my building."

"I can't believe you right now."

"Me?" he snapped. "You're just recovering from the biggest scandal of your life, and I find you publicly flirting with Anthony Dine."

"Flirting?" I wrapped my arms around my stomach. "I wasn't flirting."

"Prove me wrong, James."

"He got me a soda. We were talking. I didn't do anything wrong." I pushed my back into the corner of the seat and door, and I faced him. "In fact, I was so perfect tonight, it was almost sickening. I smiled and spoke to every person your team had introduced me to. I was the model client, and don't you dare tell me otherwise."

"And then you publicly flirted with the biggest playboy in Miami."

I was so mad, my top lip curled. "I don't think Anthony has that title. I think that one goes to you."

"Now, I've heard it all."

"Brett, women were talking about you in the ladies' room when I went in there to pee." There was so much emotion in my chest, it was hard to take a deep breath. "They were saying you brought Rebecca Andrews to your limo, so you could fuck her tonight, that they'd seen you all over town with her."

He glanced out the window, shaking his head. "They have seen me all over town with her because she's my fucking client."

"Are you sleeping with her?"

"No."

It was too dark in the back seat to see his eyes, but I wasn't sure if looking into them would tell me the truth anyway.

"I don't believe you."

"You need to quit this jealousy, James, and grow the hell up. This is my life and my business, and just because you see me talking to a woman doesn't mean I'm fucking her."

My whole body was shaking now.

"I need to grow up? You're the one who threw a fit when you caught me talking to another guy."

"Every time a different woman approached me, I saw jealousy all over your face. So, you thought you'd flirt with Anthony to get back at me. The same way you did to Abel the night you met Calvin."

It felt like he had just slapped me across the face.

"That's low."

"It's the truth," he hissed.

I turned my body toward the front, and before I took my eyes off him, I said, "That wasn't what I was doing. I ran into Anthony on my way out of the restroom, and we started talking. It was completely innocent."

"Nothing with Anthony Dine is ever innocent."

I didn't reply, and several minutes passed before he spoke again, "I didn't mean to ignore you tonight."

The feelings that flowed through me hadn't died down at all. I was hurt at what he had said. I was pissed that he hadn't given me any attention. I was jealous that women thought he was sleeping with Rebecca when I wanted him to be sleeping with me.

"Tonight didn't go the way I had planned," he added.

"What would you have done differently?" I held my breath as I waited for him to answer.

"I would have taken you all around the room, so my hands could have been on you all night."

I didn't know how to respond, so I didn't. Instead, I rested my face against the window, and I watched the SUV head toward our building.

21

BRETT

I DIDN'T CARE if Anthony Dine was loved in this city. I didn't care if he was an outstanding quarterback and a client of Jack's. He was a fucking player, and as he'd looked at James, as he'd made her laugh, and as he'd moved a piece of hair off her face, I had known the only thing he saw was a chick whose legs he was going to get in between.

There was no way in hell I was going to let that happen.

But, from the moment I'd taken James outside the gala, I'd let my frustration control my words. Because the thought of him— anyone—touching her made me fucking crazy.

Her cheeks were mine. Her lips, too.

Only my fingers were allowed to graze them.

Only my mouth was allowed anywhere near them.

When I'd told her tonight hadn't gone as planned, that was the truth. Rebecca had monopolized me for almost the entire evening but for good reason. Netflix was interested in her series. HBO was also. I'd already received emails from both networks to set up a second meeting at their headquarters, and if things continued the way I thought they would, we'd soon be in a bidding war.

But James was hurt from the way I'd handled things tonight, from the way I'd completely ignored her, and I needed to talk to her about that.

"James, listen—" My voice cut off as the driver stopped in front of our building.

James immediately got out, not waiting for him to open her door.

I was right behind her.

She stood in front of the elevators, repeatedly pressing the button until one arrived. When it did, she walked in and hit the button to her floor.

We both knew this elevator didn't go to the penthouse. That didn't stop me from getting on and moving to the back wall where I leaned against it. Now, I had the most perfect view of her ass, and it teased the hell out of me. The cutouts on her hips were calling my hands; the ones on her shoulders needed my lips.

"James..."

She didn't turn around.

She didn't respond either.

She just stared at the screen on the wall that showed what floor we were on.

When we reached the ninth, I took a step forward and another, now only inches from her. My fingers twitched for her skin. My nose wanted to graze her neck to take in her pear scent.

The door opened, and she began to walk out.

I stopped her, cupping the cutouts, my mouth pressing against her cheek, right below her ear. "Don't move."

Her body tightened as I touched it. "What do you want?"

I flipped the switch that held the elevator in place, keeping the door from closing. Then, my hand returned to her, sliding around her navel, my face in her neck. I breathed her in. "You."

"You told me that couldn't happen."

I exhaled over her shoulder. "I can't stand not having you."

"Brett, I'm so mad at you right now."

My lips went to the back of her ear. "Show me."

"Fuck you," she seethed.

"Yes," I hissed. "That's what I want." As she went to speak again, I gripped her tighter to cut her off. "Take your anger out on me." My mouth moved above her earlobe. "Show me how mad you are with your body." My fingers ran up to her ribs, teasing the bottom of her tits. "Do you know that this is all I've thought about tonight? Touching your whole body, wondering how soft your skin would feel if I peeled this dress off you." My palm pushed between her tits. "I know you were thinking about me, too, James." I could feel the war that was happening inside her. "You deserved my attention, and I should have given it to you. But you're getting it now, and my mouth is all yours. Tell me where you want it." She said nothing, so I flicked my thumb across her nipple. "Do you want it here?" She whimpered, and I traveled down until I reached her cunt, brushing the very top of it. "How about here?" I searched for the elastic, and when I didn't feel one, I said, "No panties. Did you do that for me?" More silence, but her head now rested against my chest, and I could see her mouth was open, her eyes closed. "Were you hoping I'd notice, and somewhere inside the gala, I'd slip a finger in your pussy and make you fucking scream?" I finally got the sound I wanted to hear, one that vibrated through me, so I dipped my fingers a little lower. "Is this where you want my mouth? Right here on your clit?"

"Brett..." she breathed.

With the door still open, I turned her around to face me. I felt the intensity of her stare the second it landed on me. It was animalistic, full of anger and hunger.

"You're such a fucking asshole."

I smiled from her words and moved further down her body, getting on my knees and placing my fingers on her ankles. "It's been too long since I tasted you, James."

She watched every goddamn move. Neither her eyes nor her expression changed.

"Someone could see us."

That was true, but I would hear their feet on the hardwood floor, and it would give me enough time to straighten her dress and stand up. Since I heard nothing, my hands crawled to her calves and up her thighs, circling them from front to back. I massaged my way to her ass and around to the sides of her pussy, though I never touched it.

Her inhale was loud, sharp.

"I just need a taste." I lifted her dress and held it against her stomach, my mouth right below it. I was close enough to smell her pussy but not lick it. So, I took the deepest inhale. And then I moved a few inches closer, sticking my nose in between her lips and breathing in again. "Fuck, I've missed this." With my eyes not moving from hers, I pulled my nose away to swipe my tongue across her clit. "Mmm," I growled. I spread her lips apart and lapped in between them.

"Brett...the door..."

I wasn't leaving this elevator until she came on my tongue. And hearing her say my name only made me lick harder.

I teased her entrance with two fingers until they were coated in her wetness, and then I plunged both inside, twisting up to my knuckles before pulling out and going back in. Then, using just the tip of my tongue, I flicked across the very top of her clit, going around and around before sucking it into my mouth.

She grabbed my hair between her fingers. "Oh my God."

I released the suction and traced up and down her pussy. My beard scraped against her thighs with each movement, and I knew that small amount of pain could help her build an orgasm.

It was doing just that.

Her moans became louder, the muscles in her legs tightened, and when I felt her get so fucking wet, I sucked her clit into my mouth again to give her the friction she needed and teased the end with my teeth.

Shudders pulsed through her body. "Yes, fuck, I'm coming."

Her fingers tugged my goddamn hair so hard, I thought she would rip it from my scalp. Still, I didn't stop until I knew she was far past the edge, and then I grabbed her ass and lifted her, carrying her to her apartment.

James gave me her keys, and I got us inside, taking her to the couch where I bent her over the top of it. Quickly unbuttoning and unzipping my pants, I let them drop and moved in behind her.

Her cunt was still so wet from my mouth, so I rubbed some of it over the tip of my cock and slowly plunged in.

"Fuck," I hissed, remembering how tight and how warm her pussy was.

And how she got wetter the more I stroked.

"Goddamn it, James, you feel so good," I groaned.

I needed her nipples between my fingers, so I pulled out, lifted her, and moved her to the wall. I spread her legs around me and entered her again. Using her back to hold her weight, I pinched those tiny buds.

"Harder," she begged.

I let up to sweep the ends with my thumbs before tugging them.

She moaned, "Just like that."

As I ground my hips, she tightened, squeezing my tip, and I thrust right back in.

It was my turn.

I lifted her off the wall and switched positions, so my back was now pressed against it, and I said, "Make me come."

As she held on to my shoulders and bounced on my cock, I pulled the dress over her head and unhooked the bra from behind her back, taking one of her nipples into my mouth. I bit the end, sucking it, feeling her buck every time my teeth pierced her skin.

She dug her nails into my shoulders, her back now arching, her body rising and falling, taking me in all the way.

"Faster," I ordered.

James listened.

But, this time, she kept me plunged inside while she circled her hips, my dick reaching the spot I knew she liked.

I moved on to her other nipple, sucking it so hard, she cried out, "I'm coming."

I could feel it.

She was pulsing around my cock, her body frozen as the pleasure worked its way through. Making sure she felt every wave, I grabbed her hips and pumped into her, getting her to scream even louder. And, as she started to quiet just a little, I pounded out my orgasm, shooting my cum inside her, her clenched pussy sucking out every drop.

When we both stilled, I stayed inside her and moved us over to the couch. She was panting. Her hair was wild, her skin red from all the places my beard and teeth had roughed her up. I felt more wetness begin to leak on my balls, and I lifted her just a little, so I could see myself pouring out of her.

It was the hottest fucking sight.

Me mixed with her.

I watched it pool over the base of my dick, and once it stopped, I lifted her again and carried her into the bedroom where I whispered, "Shower," into her ear.

22

JAMES

Eve: There'd better be a damn good reason you didn't text me last night.
Me: Why are you awake? It's, like, four in the morning there.
Eve: It's Max's fault. He kept me up all night.
Me: He's not even there.
Eve: Duh. Video sex, remember?
Me: You've been having video sex alllll this time? The gala has been over for hours.
Eve: That man is insatiable.
Me: Then, you're perfect for each other.
Eve: Answer my question, bitch, and tell me why you're awake this early.
Me: Brett stayed the night.
Eve: And?
Me: We hooked up.
Eve: AND?
Me: I'm a bundle of questions, and it's making me crazy.
Eve: Have you asked any of them?
Me: No, I couldn't. His tongue was too busy...

Eve: God, I love him.

Me: You're supposed to be on my side.

Eve: I am. I just approve of his tongue when it comes to my best friend's vag. Seriously though, you need to have a conversation with him. We can't have you crazy, especially not now. We need you sane, so we can get you back into auditions.

Me: I already know what he's going to say. Same thing as last time —we can't do this again; I have to focus on your career, so I can't fuck you and be your agent at the same time.

Eve: Maybe he'll surprise you.

Me: He did that last night when he said I was acting jealous and retaliating, like I had the night I slept with Calvin. But, Eve, I wasn't. Anthony Dine was at the gala, and we were just talking. I hadn't sought him out, and I definitely hadn't done what Brett accused me of.

Eve: Anthony Dine? He's such a fucking player, James. I'm glad you didn't do more than just talk to him.

23

BRETT

WHEN I OPENED MY EYES, I was almost blinded by the goddamn sun coming in through the windows. To block all the light, I immediately rolled onto my stomach and pulled a pillow over the back of my head. This was the reason I never left my blinds open before I went to bed, so I couldn't understand how I'd forgotten last night.

Last night, last night...

Slowly, the details started to come back to me.

The reason the blinds were open was because they weren't on my windows, and I wasn't in my bed.

I'd stayed the night at James's.

I'd fucked her against the wall, and we'd taken a shower. Then, I'd fucked her once more before we both passed out.

Now, as I felt my morning wood grind into the mattress, I wanted her again.

I stretched my arm to the other side of the bed and searched for that warm, gorgeous body. But, as I reached the end, all I felt were sheets and a blanket.

Is she on the other side?

I gradually rolled onto my back and looked across the bed. She wasn't in it. That was when I heard the sound of the shower and saw light coming out from underneath the bathroom door.

I got up and was pleased to find it unlocked. I went inside, taking James's toothbrush from the holder and covering it in toothpaste. I did a quick brush, and then I stuck it back, walking over to the shower. The large walk-in was constructed from a series of walls that weaved to the right and left before opening into the large space.

Since there wasn't any glass and her back was facing me, she hadn't seen me coming. And I knew she hadn't heard me because, when I wrapped my arms around her stomach, she jolted and shrieked, "Brett!"

"It's just me." As I kissed across her back, my cock pressed against the lower part of it. Once I covered all the skin there, I moved up her neck and stopped at her jaw. "Why did you get up so early? It's Saturday. You could have slept in, and I could have woken you with this." I ground my tip into the top of her ass and gently bit into her shoulder.

She put her hands on top of mine and tried to pull my fingers off her navel. "Because that's all you want from me, Brett."

I turned her around to face me, searching her eyes and seeing that the hardness had returned—the side she'd shown me in the SUV.

"What's wrong?"

"Do you remember what you said to me in the conference room the day I signed with you? Let me fill you in, in case you've forgotten. You told me nothing could happen between us. You were only going to be my agent, and that was it. Then, you saw me talking to another guy, and you freaked out, took me home, and ate me out in the elevator."

"You liked it."

"Brett—"

"We had this argument last night, James. I'm not having it again."

She shook her head, her arms crossing over her tits. "No, we didn't because this argument isn't about the way you acted at the gala or the things you said to me in the SUV. This is about us. You can't just fuck me every time you're horny, Brett. You have no idea what that does to me emotionally. You treat me like I'm just some thing you can play with whenever you want, and it's not fair."

"I treat you like a client."

"Then, what the hell was last night?" Her hands dropped, so she could squeeze the tips of my fingers. "And why are you touching me right now?" She looked down. "And why is your dick hard if I'm just your client?"

"Because you're standing in front of me, naked, and you have one of the best bodies I've ever seen."

"So, it's not even me that you want; it's my body. Awesome. That makes me feel even worse."

I was losing my patience. She knew I wanted both. I had no idea why she was even questioning it. "What do you want from me, James?"

She took a few steps back to put some space between us and said, "I want an answer."

"To what?"

"To what we are. To your feelings about me. To why you slept with me."

"I can't have this fucking conversation."

I turned around and marched my ass out of the shower, the water from my body soaking the tiles by my feet. I went to the sink where I gripped the edge and took a few deep breaths while I stared at my reflection in the mirror.

What the fuck is this girl doing to me?

She wanted something I didn't give to women because I

never got that far with them. I certainly hadn't earned the bach-elor title by jumping from relationship to relationship.

But can I even give her what she's looking for?

I let those thoughts simmer as I took a few more breaths, and then I went back into the shower. This time, she was facing me, and the hurt on her face pounded straight to my chest.

"I needed a second," I told her.

"Why? Because you didn't want to hurt me? I can handle it, Brett. Even if it means you're just using me for sex and you don't feel anything for me, I just want to hear the truth."

Each emotion that blasted across her face hit me even harder.

My goddamn thoughts were still all over the place.

When I'd told her I couldn't be her agent and fuck her at the same time, I'd meant it.

But seeing her with Anthony had made me seethe. It'd made me realize how much I wanted her. It'd made me fear that she would try to move on even though it was what she needed to do.

It'd made me want to give her a reminder of how good I was. So, I had.

And, now, whenever she thought about another guy, I wanted her to remember what had happened in that elevator and wonder if his tongue could ever compare to mine. If he could fuck her like I had when I held her against the wall.

That was because I'd convinced myself that she was my client, therefore I couldn't have her. She was too young. She was in the middle of a public relations nightmare, and being with me would only make that worse. We had to stay focused on what was best for her career, and that was staying away from me personally.

I told myself that every goddamn day.

And, every time I got close to her—when my hands started to reach toward her body, when my nose searched the air for her scent—I would repeat those thoughts in my head.

But I was tired of telling myself I couldn't have her.

My fingers clenched at my sides, keeping them busy so that they wouldn't move forward and circle her waist. "I've been trying to protect you, James." My voice was the softest it had ever been, and I didn't recognize the sound of it.

"From what?"

I looked down at the drain, my eyes closing, my head shaking, before I glanced up and said, "Me."

There were so many emotions on her face, I wasn't sure which was the strongest. "That decision isn't up to you."

"That's what you hired me for. To make decisions like that."

"No. I hired you to be in charge of my career, but you're not allowed to manage my heart, and it makes me furious that you would even try." She put her hand over her chest. "Every decision has been taken away from me. Don't take that one, too."

"James—"

"When I try to process all the signs—you know, that you got jealous over Anthony, that I saw you jerking off on the plane only minutes after leaving me in my chair, and the way you always look at me during meetings—I start to think you want me and that you have feelings you're just trying to hide. But then I rack my brain, trying to figure out why you don't act on anything and why you leave before something can happen between us. I don't want to question it anymore. I just want to know. Do you want me or not?"

"What you're asking for isn't a simple yes or no." I run my hands through my hair, pulling at the ends. "This is going to affect your career, and I cannot let that happen."

"How?" she bellowed. "You have my career under control. The gala was one of the best nights I'd had in a long time. Your team made sure everything went perfectly from the red carpet to the introductions. So, don't use that as an excuse."

"I'm talking about if people found out about us."

"Who's going to tell them? It certainly isn't going to be me."

She wanted to keep us a secret.

I hadn't expected that.

I backed up until I felt the wall behind me, the freezing tiles cooling down my body while the hot water splashed over my chest. I pushed the back of my head across the grout lines as I thought about my next move. Once I told her the truth, I couldn't take it back. Things would change between us—again. And I'd have to find a way to make this work because her career would always have to come first—at least while I was representing her.

I glanced down at her legs, wondering if I was making the biggest mistake of my life or the smartest. Wondering if I would regret this somehow. Wondering if my best friends would think I'd lost my goddamn mind.

It didn't matter.

She had to know.

I continued to look up until I reached her eyes and finally said, "I want you."

"Then, stop fucking with my emotions, and come and get me."

The demanding side of her was so fucking hot.

I pushed myself off the wall and moved a little closer.

"I'm giving myself to you, Brett. All of me. I'd better get that from you in return because I don't want to hear any more excuses."

I took another step. "We have to be so careful. Do you hear me? The public cannot find out about us or—"

"Brett, no one is going to tell them."

One final step, and then I reached her.

"It's just us. The way it should have been since the night you took me home from the bar."

I ran my hand around the back of her head and fisted her

hair, pulling her face closer until her eyes closed and our lips connected.

This kiss was different.

It was deeper. Stronger. It was a taste I needed before I said, "You're mine."

I'd fought this feeling for too long. I'd sometimes ask her to come into my office for no reason, just so I could be around her. When I got home from work, my hand would fist my cock with thoughts of her in my head to make it feel like I was getting a piece of her.

I'd hoped the want would go away.

It hadn't because James was who I wanted.

Whom I needed to be with.

And, now, she was finally mine.

"God, you made this so hard." She laughed.

I rested the tip of my nose on hers and took a breath. "I want what's best for you, and I still don't know if I'm that person."

"Let me decide that."

My lips moved to her forehead, and they kissed the center of it. "This doesn't mean that, when it comes to your career, I'm going to give you any control. I'm not; I assure you of that. There's a chance every business decision I make will affect us personally. I'm warning you now; it can get complicated, and there will be days you're probably going to hate me."

"I'm not worried."

I cupped her ass and lifted her into the air, feeling her legs wrap around my waist. "We have to be careful."

After she finished kissing my cheek, she said, "I lost everything once. I won't risk that again."

I turned her around and pushed her back against the wall. "I promise you one thing; no matter what happens between us, I'm going to do everything in my power to get back everything you've lost, and nothing will change that."

"I know." Her lips hovered in front of mine. "You came in this shower for a reason. Now, put your lips on mine, Brett, and fuck me already."

"Mmm," I growled, knowing there was no way I could say no to that.

24

JAMES

IT HAD ONLY BEEN a week since the gala, and my life in Miami had already changed so much. Yesterday, I'd had lunch with three of the women I'd met there that night, and I had several more scheduled for next week. Brett's team had been receiving multiple phone calls a day with invites for me to attend events, and my evenings were booking up with charity engagements. Pictures of me were circling the internet, showing me dressed in the outfits Eve had chosen with short blurbs that described where I was and the people I'd interacted with.

The public was starting to be a little kinder.

What they didn't know was that Brett and I were secretly dating.

No one knew that, except for Eve and Max, the only two people we'd decided to tell because we figured we'd be spending time with them together.

I'd been so unsure about moving to Florida, especially when I'd first gotten here and had nothing to do, but I was definitely starting to feel more comfortable. Miami gave me privacy that I hadn't had in LA. The paparazzi didn't stalk the restaurants and beaches. I could go to the pool and travel in and out of my building, and I didn't have to cover my face. I was making so much progress at the gym, my strength building more each time I went. And I was taking daily acting lessons from a private coach and working with a voice therapist to improve my tone.

Miami was good to me, and it was good for me.

I was establishing a routine, and that was why, when the police detective called and said he wanted to meet with me, I was so hesitant to return to LA.

Brett had said the timing was perfect. He had a meeting there, and Max had to go see a client, so the three of us flew together.

From the second the plane landed, I was on the lookout for cameras. I knew, if the paparazzi caught sight of me, they wouldn't leave me alone, speculating why I was in town, making up stories about my comeback. Things were just starting to get better for me, and I didn't want any rumors out there. So, I was relieved when, on our way to the police station, Brett got a text from Max. It said his plans had changed, and we wouldn't be staying the night like we'd thought, but we would be heading back east sometime this evening.

The less time I spent in this city, the better.

And, hopefully, the quicker my anxiety would die down because I was a bundle of nerves as we arrived at LAPD. Brett and I were led into a private room and told the detective would be in shortly. It took several minutes for him to join us. As he did, he sat on the other side of the table and placed a folder in front of him.

"Thanks for coming in, Miss Ryne," the detective said. "I know it was a long trip for you."

"No problem." I clenched my hands together underneath the table and felt how slick and sweaty they were.

The detective opened the folder and read the first few pages before our eyes connected. "I'd like to update you on where things stand. We sent the video through our forensic department, and they weren't able to find any distinguishable marks on the man in the video. Unfortunately, whoever edited it did a thorough job. We scanned the hotel's surveillance tapes several more times, even running it through our face recognition software, and we still haven't been able to find anyone who fits Mr. Parker's description, nor have we seen you on any of the footage. My analysts searched the internet and couldn't find the source of the leak, where the video was uploaded, or how it got distributed. And, at this point, you've seen every Calvin Parker we have in our system, and there hasn't been a positive match, therefore we have to believe that's not his name." He crossed his arms over the table and leaned forward. "Miss Ryne, we're at a dead end."

I glanced at Brett, and there was so much anger filling his face. I knew he'd been looking into things on his end and not gotten any further than the police.

"I called you in for two reasons. First, I need to know if you can give us any more information. Anything that can help with our search. Maybe a detail you forgot the first time we met, like a tattoo hidden somewhere or a birthmark, the kind of car he drove, something he might have said about where he lives or works."

I took a deep breath and ran the whole night through my head, trying to come up with something I hadn't remembered before.

The party had started early in the afternoon, and I'd had several drinks as I watched Sophia and Abel make out. The vodka had gone down so easily, and since I'd moved that day, I hadn't eaten much, and the liquor had hit me hard.

Calvin and I had left the party fairly early. He'd had a driver waiting in the driveway, and we'd climbed in the back of the SUV —a make and color that was like every other one I'd ridden in. Then, he'd dropped us off at the hotel. I never saw more than the profile of the driver's face, and I couldn't even recall the color of his hair.

When we'd arrived at the hotel, we had gone in through a side door, which told me Calvin already had a key, and the room was on the first floor, so we didn't have to walk through the lobby or take an elevator.

I could see Calvin's face, but even that was a little fuzzy. He had no tattoos, no birthmarks that I had seen, no piercings, and nothing about his looks stood out to the point where he would be noticed in a roomful of people.

He was plain.

But that didn't bother me, and it certainly hadn't at that time.

When I'd left the next morning, he had been sleeping on his stomach, so I hadn't really gotten another good look at him.

And that was all the time we'd spent together. There hadn't been much talking, not many questions asked, certainly not a moment where he had opened up to me.

I had nothing to give to the detective that would help catch that asshole.

"I've told you everything," I said.

It was hard to say that out loud, admitting how much of a mistake I'd made, one that had cost me so much.

"The other reason I asked you to come in is because I have some mug shots I'd like you to look at. Some of these men work for the hotel in Malibu, and some work for the transportation companies around town that could have driven you to the hotel. Let me know if you recognize any of them."

I took the stack of papers he'd pulled out from the folder, and I flipped through each page, focusing on their eyes and hair and if they showed any teeth. There were four photographs per sheet, and I spent plenty of time staring at each one.

When I got to the last page, I shook my head. "None of those guys look familiar."

He scratched his nail over the desk, chipping away at what looked like a piece of paint. "We discussed witnesses the last time we chatted. I know you checked with Eve Kennedy, and she wasn't able to identify him either. What about anyone else?"

"I reached out to a few other friends who were there, and no one remembers him. They had all been drinking, too, and so many people had been there that it was hard to keep track of anyone."

The only people I hadn't asked were Abel and Sophia. The thought of doing that made me sick. But there was a chance they could have seen Calvin, and at some point, I needed to find the courage to talk to them.

"Without any more leads or evidence, I'm going to have to close the case," the detective said. "Of course, if you remember something or new information is presented, I can certainly reopen it."

There was a lump in my throat that was bigger than the detective's hand.

I'd come all the way here for him to tell me we were at a standstill.

"Are you sure?" I asked. "There really isn't anything else that can be done?"

"I'm sorry, Miss Ryne. We've exhausted all our resources."

As I opened my mouth, with not a clue as to what would come out of it, I felt Brett's hand on my shoulder, urging me to stand.

"Thanks for your help, Detective," Brett said. "James and I will be in touch if anything new comes about."

"I hope you will," the detective said, moving to our side of the table to shake our hands. "Off the record, I have a daughter your age, and the thought of that happening to her doesn't sit well. Personally, I'd like to nail that bastard, so keep thinking, and let me know if you come up with anything."

"Will do," Brett replied, now squeezing my shoulder.

I finally got to my feet, following the detective down the hallway and out the side of the station where we immediately got into an SUV.

Brett had to take a phone call, so I took out my phone and typed Eve a text.

Me: Just left LAPD. They have nothing. The case is closed unless something else comes up.

Eve: Ugh. I was afraid you would say that.

Me: You still don't remember anything?

Eve: I can't picture him, babe. Trust me, I've been trying. How's LA? I can't believe you're there, and I'm not.

Me: You know I'd stay longer if that meant seeing you, but honestly, I'm kinda relieved to get out of here. Something about this place doesn't feel like home anymore.

Eve: I'll be in Miami soon.

Me: Miss you.

Eve: More than you know.

I looked up from the screen just as Brett got off the phone, and I saw we were headed in the opposite direction of the airport. He hadn't told me where I would be waiting while he went to his meeting, so I said, "Are you bringing me with you?"

"Yes." He reached across the seat and put his hand on my thigh. "You did good back there."

"I'm so furious with myself."

"Baby, there's nothing we can do to change what happened. We just have to keep looking until we find that motherfucker."

That was the first time he'd called me that, and despite how angry I was, I couldn't stop myself from smiling.

"You've done everything you can," he added. "Now, we have

to wait for something to unfold. And it will, I promise you, because no one in this town can keep their mouth shut."

As I nodded, I saw that his phone was ringing again, and Scarlett's name was on the screen. "Go ahead and talk to her; it's okay."

He kept his hand on my leg and answered the call as I scrolled through social media. The first picture I came across was of Abel and Sophia. It had been taken yesterday as they were walking out of a furniture store, the shot showing a close-up of her diamond with the headline, *Decorating the Nursery?*

It didn't matter if she was pregnant or redecorating or adding an addition on to the house; I still owned half of it. I didn't want it; it was just something I'd been avoiding since we broke up.

There was no reason to avoid it anymore.

I hit the button for my email and opened a new one, which I addressed to my attorney, and I began to type.

CAN YOU PLEASE DRAW UP THE PAPERWORK TO HAVE ABEL
BUY ME OUT OF OUR HOUSE?
ALL I'M LOOKING FOR IS THE FAIR MARKET VALUE.
I'D LIKE TO GET THIS WRAPPED UP AS SOON AS POSSIBLE.
THANK YOU.

As I glanced up, I noticed we were pulling up to a gate and stopping in front of the call box on the side.

The driver rolled down his window and said into the intercom, "Mr. Young and Miss Ryne here to see Mr. Anderson."

My eyes moved to Brett. "Why did he say my name?"

"Scarlett, I've got to go." He hung up, and his fingers tightened on my thigh. "The meeting is for both of us."

"Both of us?" I looked out the window and saw the curved driveway and the massive house that sat in the back of it. "Where are we? And who's Mr. Anderson—" I cut myself off as a thought came into my mind. One that caused my hands to shake. "This isn't Ralph Anderson's house, is it?"

Brett nodded as the SUV came to a halt in front of the grand entrance.

"And you didn't think it was important to mention that we were meeting with the largest director in the world?" I gazed down at the clothes I had on. I'd worn nothing to stand out, only a pair of jeans, a tank top, and a small sweater. "I'm not dressed for this. I—"

"Relax. It's an informal meeting, and the reason I didn't tell you was because I didn't want you freaking out like you're doing right now."

"Goddamn right I'm freaking out. How could you do this to me? This could be one of the biggest moments of my life, and I'm not prepared." I looked at the house, seeing a butler come out the front and approach my door. "I can't go in there. I'm not ready."

"Look at me," he growled. I did as he'd asked, and he said, "You've been waiting your whole life for this. You're ready, and I believe in you. Now, go show that man why you're the best fucking actress in Hollywood."

25

BRETT

IT HAD ONLY TAKEN Henry a day to reach out to me after the gala. I appreciated how fast he'd worked. I also appreciated the monster connection he'd hooked me up with. Ralph Anderson was a guy I'd been fucking dying to get in the same room with since I became an agent. He was the most talented director in the industry, and he held the record for the most awards. His films weren't just stories; they were experiences that captivated you so hard, you forgot you were watching a movie.

Ralph didn't meet with agents. He didn't hold auditions either. His team called the actors Ralph wanted to work with, and private auditions were then held to make sure it was a good fit. The only way to get into an Anderson film was to be the best in the business and hope to hell someone from his team noticed you.

Not one of my clients had gotten that phone call.

So, when I'd spoken to Ralph's team and found out he wanted to meet immediately, I had known I had to get us on a plane. The call from the detective couldn't have worked out more perfectly because it meant I didn't have to tell James about Ralph until we were outside his house. Had I told her, she would have been a mess during the flight and at the police station, and I didn't want that kind of pressure weighing on her.

It was a good decision because, as I looked at her now, seconds before the butler reached her door, I was worried she was going to throw up.

Quickly, I lifted my hand off her leg and brushed my fingers across the back of her neck, giving her a last bit of encouragement. "Fucking kill it, baby," I whispered and then moved away from her, so the butler didn't see.

"I'm going to kill you," she said softly over her shoulder, sliding out of the back once the door opened.

I walked behind her, following the butler into a large sitting room, and took the chair next to James's.

"Can I get you anything to drink?" the butler asked.

"Water, please," James said.

He looked at me, and I nodded, silently asking for the same.

I was close enough to see every breath she inhaled, how her chest rose and fell, how her hands fidgeted in her lap. She crossed her legs, and her fingers moved to the ankle of her jeans, running her nails across the hem.

She was nervous as hell.

"James," I said and waited for her to glance at me before I added, "stop thinking about why you're here. Stop worrying about what you're going to say. I just want you to think about what you were doing around midnight last night."

In case the cameras in the corners of the room were able to pick up sound, I didn't want to say she had been on her back at midnight with her legs spread and my face between them. But it was around that time and over the next thirty minutes that my tongue had been on her cunt, and she'd been screaming through each orgasm I gave her.

The expression on her face told me she remembered.

But it was gone the second the butler returned with two glasses of water. He set them on the side table next to our chairs.

As he left, Ralph came right in and said, "I didn't mean to keep you waiting."

He walked over to me first, and I stood to shake his hand, surprised by how young he appeared in person. He didn't attend industry parties, just award shows, so I'd only seen him on camera, and it had aged him older than fifty.

"It's a pleasure," I said, taking in his grip that was as firm as mine.

"My golfing buddy, Henry, doesn't praise many people, and he had some nice things to say about you. Therefore, I knew you were someone I had to meet."

"Thank you for giving me the time."

He released my hand and moved over to James. "It's nice to meet you, Miss Ryne. I was just upstairs in my screening room, reviewing your last release."

She surrounded his hand with both of hers. "Wow. Thank you. I'm a huge fan, and I'm so honored you were willing to meet me."

She sounded humble, but I could still hear the anxiety in her tone.

Neither of us sat until Ralph walked to the other side of the coffee table where he took a seat on the couch. That was when the butler came back in and placed a can of soda in front of him.

"Tell me something, James," Ralph said once we were alone. "What type of role are you looking for?"

She paused, and I could tell she was thinking about his question. "I want one that challenges me."

She could do better than that.

"You haven't been challenged so far in your career?" he asked.

She was thinking again but finally said, "Not emotionally, no."

I wanted to reach across the space between us and shake the hell out of her. Her short answers weren't going to impress him. They were flat, generic. They showed him nothing.

"Explain," he said.

And, again, she stalled before slowly parting her lips. "The roles I've taken had me act with such basic human emotions—love and sadness. I'm not opposed to either, of course, but I want to dig deeper. I want to read a script and feel the full range, my chest pounding, my tears streaming, my stomach churning. Angst and anger and pain and courage. I've experienced them all in my life, and I want to channel those memories. I want to feel the script. I want to become the character. But I don't want to be known as an actress who can only do love and sadness."

That was my fucking girl.

She was finally turning it around.

Ralph crossed his legs and put his pointer fingers in a steeple under his nose. "About ten years ago, I released a movie called *Burnt Away*. It's about a team of firefighters who go into a high-rise that's on fire. Once they get inside, the entire building explodes. It was an act of terrorism, and only two out of the twenty-five survive."

"The sole female on the team and the rookie were the only ones who made it out alive," she said.

"You've seen it."

She smiled. "It's one of my favorites."

Ralph's eyes narrowed. He was looking at her differently now.

I was, too, with so much fucking pride in my eyes.

"It took me months to cast that role," he said. "Everyone I called in wasn't right for the part. I needed someone to forget that there were cameras, that there was lighting, that there were lines to read. I needed that person to live in the moment. When actors came in, I made them audition the hardest scene in the film. The one where the female was in the hospital, and she'd just gotten her hands treated for third-degree burns. As she processed what had just happened to her and her squad, she moved into the corner of the room, and she rocked in a ball, losing herself, screaming out in so much pain."

I remembered the scene well. The actress had won an Oscar.

"May I be frank?" James asked.

I wanted to smile but didn't.

"Please," he said.

"I heard the pain in her sobs, and I saw it on her lips, but it didn't make it all the way to her eyes. It stopped at her cheeks and didn't go further."

His hands dropped, and he rested them on his knee. "You're right."

She had balls, and I wanted to fucking kiss her for it.

"She did a wonderful job," James added, "but her eyes lacked emotion almost the entire film."

"You're right again." He stared at her, and I would kill to know what he was thinking. "Show me your version."

"Right now?"

He nodded. "Yes."

I knew our meeting would be short. I had a feeling it would only take a few minutes before he knew if James would fit into one of his roles.

I knew this was the moment that, if she nailed it, would change her future.

I felt the pressure in my chest, so I could only fucking imagine how heavy it was for her.

Slowly, James held out her hands and gazed at them like she'd never seen them before. Her fingers shook and twitched, her mouth opening as she moved her hands around her face, checking them at every angle.

She gasped, the air getting caught, and a choking sound released from her throat.

She slapped her hands on the armrests, screaming as they hit the wood, the pain so great that her ass fell from the chair. She landed hard, crying out once more, and tumbled forward until her palms banged on the floor.

"*Nooo.*"

It wasn't a scream. It was an emotion that came out, and it followed her as she crawled to the corner of the fireplace before falling once again on her ass.

Her body rocked.

Her eyes widened.

Tears streamed so goddamn fast, I wanted to wipe them away.

"They're gone," she whispered through sobs.

She might have been talking about the firefighters who had been lost in the explosion, but James was pulling from the time she'd lived in her closet, her career gone, her naked body exposed to the world.

I saw that in her face. I heard it in her voice.

It reflected in her fucking eyes.

She didn't need a script. She didn't need a camera or lights or a set.

This was what she was meant to do, and she gave it everything she had.

When she finished, when there was no air left in her lungs, when the camera would have zoomed out for the next shot, she wiped her face and finally looked at the two of us.

No one spoke for several minutes until Ralph said, "It's too bad you were just a young kid when I casted that role. Had the actress done what you just did there, *Burnt Away* would have been my favorite movie, too."

I watched her swallow, and then I saw the shock register across her face.

"There's a difference between someone who's studied their craft and someone who was born with natural talent. I've worked with both, but natural is a rare find. I've put some of the most educated actors into roles no larger than a walk-on because that's what they deserve. But not you, Miss Ryne. You're raw. You're natural. What's holding you back is life. Once you get that part figured out, you'll be unstoppable. Mark my words."

Jesus fucking Christ.

I ran my fingers through my beard to hide the smile on my mouth.

"It's time for me to go," Ralph said and stood.

James thanked him, and I did as well, shaking his hand like a goddamn robot because I still couldn't believe his reaction to her. As soon as he walked out, the butler appeared, and he took us down the hall and toward the front door.

Once we climbed into the back of the SUV, James turned toward me with tears in her eyes.

Real ones.

Ones that had come from happiness, not because she was in a hospital room with burned hands.

"Brett, what the hell just happened?"

I shook my head, licking across my bottom lip, thinking of the ways I was going to fucking devour her on the plane. "You just killed it, baby."

26

JAMES

"TO ONE OF the most incredible performances I've ever seen,"
Brett said, holding his champagne glass in front of mine as we sat
in the corner of a restaurant. "For blowing Ralph Anderson's
goddamn mind. For knowing your shit and studying your craft
even though you were born a natural." He nibbled the side of his
bottom lip while his legs surrounded one of mine under the table.
"I'm so fucking proud of you right now."

Before we clinked glasses, I added, "For having the best agent
in the entire world." I lowered my voice, so the tables nearby
couldn't hear me. "Whom I'm also lucky enough to be sleeping
with. Cheers." We touched flutes, and I took a sip. "Seriously,
Brett, how did you make that meeting happen?"

"It happened. That's all that matters."

"Hard-ass."

"I'm going to be so fucking hard on your ass when we get on
that plane tonight."

I laughed just as the waitress appeared at our table.

"What can I get you guys to eat?" she asked.

"Is your mom in the kitchen?" Brett inquired.

"Yes, and I know she'll make your favorite. I don't even have to ask her."

He shut the menu, grabbed mine, and handed them to the waitress. "We'll take two." He looked at me. "Trust me."

I nodded at the both of them, and once she left the table, I said, "I didn't think we'd be able to go out to eat in LA without being seen. Thanks for bringing me here. It feels so date-ish."

"It is a date."

"It's a wait-for-Max-to-be-done-with-his-meeting-so-we-don't-have-to-sit-on-the-plane kind of date."

"That's still a fucking date, James."

I laughed again and looked around the room at the pictures of Greece that were framed on the walls, all places I'd traveled to over the years. Wine corks and grape vines decorated the ceiling. This was the cutest little Mediterranean restaurant I'd ever been to.

"I never even knew this street existed, so how did you find this place?"

"The guys, Scarlett, and I were right out of college, poor as hell, and just starting our careers. We all lived together right down the street in a two-bedroom apartment. We used to come here almost every night for soup. It was all we could afford. The owner, who's the chef, felt so bad, she used to give us loaves of bread to take home and whatever daily specials hadn't sold. She was so good to us. Now, whenever I'm in town, I stop in. The other guys do, too. The food is some of the best I've had, and it's safe to bring clients here because the paparazzi don't stalk this area."

"I like hearing stories like that."

"You'll like the food even better."

I smiled. "I mean, about you." I shifted my legs under the table, my foot now pressed against the side of his thigh. Not only was the restaurant paparazzi-proof, but my movements were also hidden by the long tablecloth. "Did Max say when we were supposed to meet him at the plane?"

Brett had called him on our way here, and their conversation was short. I'd only heard Brett's side, which told me nothing.

He shook his head. "He was just finishing up with a meeting and then going to grab some food with a client. I bet we'll be there around the same time."

The waitress came to our table with a bread basket. I unwrapped the napkin that covered it, grabbed a roll, and dipped it in some oil.

"Wow," I groaned, covering my mouth.

"I have fucking dreams about these olive rolls." He took one for himself and swirled it around in the oil.

"I don't even like olives." I swallowed and immediately took another bite. "How do we get her to open another location in Miami?"

He stared at me for several seconds with a strange grin on his face. "A place in Miami, huh?"

I shrugged. "Wouldn't you like that?"

"I'm wondering why you would want one there."

"Because I live there, Brett."

"For now."

"Well, yes, but who knows when I'll be returning to LA."

"The point is, you'll be returning."

I wrapped my hand around the stem of the glass and watched the bubbles pop on the surface of the champagne. Then, slowly, I met his eyes again. "Why do I feel like we're having a deeper conversation than one about your favorite restaurant opening in Florida?"

He shook his head, and then his eyes moved to a spot behind me, his fingers now gripping the edge of the table. "Goddamn it."

"Brett—"

My voice was cut off when I heard him add, *"Fuuuck."*

"What's wrong? Did I upset you?"

His stare moved back to me. "James, I didn't know."

"Know what? What are you talking about?"

He breathed several times and finally said, "Max never told me whom he was meeting with or that he was bringing her here."

"Max?" The look on Brett's face made me turn around. That was when my chest started to hurt, and my pulse began to throb in my neck. "What the fuck?" I heard myself hiss.

Sophia Sully was standing at the door with Max.

Brett's Max.

Eve's fucking Max.

I faced Brett again. "What is she doing here with him?" I barely recognized the anger flooding my voice. "I will kill her for trying to hook up with my best friend's guy—"

"That's not what she's doing, James. Max represents Sophia. She's been his client for a few years."

"He what?"

I gazed over my shoulder, and Sophia's stare caught mine. Her top lip curled, and her lids narrowed. The feelings we had for each other were certainly mutual.

Not able to look at her for another second, I glanced over at Max, who was standing next to her. He gave me a silent apology before he steered Sophia toward the other side of the room where the hostess was seating them.

With my attention back on Brett, I said, "Why didn't you tell me?"

"I didn't think it was important."

"You didn't think it was important to tell me that my ex's fiancée was represented by your company and your best friend?"

I didn't know what angered me more—having to share the same air as her during a night that was supposed to be about Brett and me or Brett not telling me that Max was her agent.

I leaned back in my chair, my arms covering my chest, unable to even look at the rest of the roll on my plate because the thought of putting it in my mouth made me queasy.

"You're mad."

I sighed and uncrossed my legs to slide them back to my side of the table. "I just want to get out of here and get away from her."

"James, what happened between you and Sophia?"

I thought back to the day when I'd moved out of the house I had shared with Abel. He had been filming that morning, but Sophia had been home. All her stuff was already there—in the same places where I'd kept my things. Her clothes were in my closet. Her toothbrush was in my bathroom. Her fucking birth control was on my dresser. She'd taken all my things out of the bedroom and thrown them into the garage. The only items she hadn't put in there was my furniture, which I'd told Abel he could keep. She'd followed me around the house, talking nonstop, spitting so much hatred that I'd cried the entire drive back to the house I rented.

"She told me she'd been sleeping with Abel for months, and she gave me every detail. Like how she would suck his cock while he was on the phone with me, how she'd lived with him when he was filming in Chicago. She knew about the times he'd turned me down for sex because he didn't want to cheat on her. Her! Can you believe that? We were the couple, not him and Sophia." I felt a knot move into my throat, and tears threatened to fill my eyes. I wouldn't let them. I wouldn't give her the satisfaction of making me cry again. "She knew secrets about me that only Abel knew and things we'd gone through during our relationship that he never should have shared with her. She basically tried to crush me emotionally. And she did."

"She's a cunt."

"But, Brett, she got us to break up. She got me out of the

house we had bought together. She got everything she wanted." I pulled my napkin off my lap and twisted it around my fingers. "I reached out to Abel so many times before that night in Malibu. Even though we weren't together anymore, I just wanted to hear his voice, to find out what I had done wrong. I couldn't process that the man I'd been with since I was thirteen was no longer in my life." I stopped to take a sip of my champagne. "Sophia must have seen my messages because she sent me one from her phone that showed screenshots of my texts to him, and she threatened to share them on her social media accounts to show the world how desperate I was. I didn't want that to happen, so I gave up."

That was only a couple of weeks before I'd moved out. But she had brought up the texts, too, while I was carrying my things to my car.

I hadn't spoken to either of them since.

"James, the guy she got is a piece of fucking trash. He was only relevant and popular because he was dating you. The best roles he's had are low-budget comedies, and he only landed those because he has a set of abs. You were always too good for him, and he knows that."

Brett was only trying to make me feel better, and it helped, but I had loved Abel so much, I never cared about what roles he got or how well he did. But I was sure that was something Abel had cared about. He was so competitive. If I compared the movies I'd landed and the contracts I'd signed, I would always win. And I was sure that had bothered him.

The waitress stopped by our table with several plates.

Before she could set them down, Brett stopped her with, "Change of plans. Can we get these wrapped up, so we can take them to go?"

"No problem, Brett."

He waited until we were alone again to say, "We're going to continue this date on the plane."

"I—"

"Don't fight me on this. This is your night, and we're going to celebrate."

27

BRETT

WE'D ALREADY FINISHED our dinner on the plane, and we were relaxing on the couch, watching a movie, when Max boarded.

He wasn't inside more than a few steps when his hands went in the air, and he said, "I didn't know you guys were eating there. I should have asked before I went. That was fucking stupid of me."

I looked at James. She had a blanket up to her neck, and her legs were resting over mine. When we'd returned to the plane with our food, we'd had a long talk about Ralph and the events she had coming up, and I'd tried so goddamn hard to get her mind off Sophia. As far as I could tell, it had worked.

Until now.

"It's not your fault," she said. "I just couldn't eat in the same room as her."

Max sat in the middle of the plane, closest to the couch. "Sophia's a client. She's not a friend. And my relationship with you is different, but that doesn't mean I'm going to listen to you talk about her. You're allowed to hate each other. I just can't get involved."

"I get it." James played with my hand as it rested on her lap. "Eve doesn't know you work with Sophia."

"I haven't told her or even mentioned Sophia's name," he said. "But I guess there's a chance she could have heard. It's not something I hide."

"Oh, trust me, she doesn't know. Because, if she did, she'd have flipped her shit, and she certainly would have brought it up to you by now."

"It's like that?"

James nodded. "Eve is the most loyal person I know. When she hears this, she won't be happy. Expect an earful; I'm just warning you."

I sighed. "Jesus Christ, you women."

"It's how we work," she said, giving me a side smile. "You love us for it."

Now, that was a fucking statement I chose not to respond to.

"Are you going to tell her?" Max asked.

James shook her head. "That's all on you."

"Good. I'll take care of it." He took his suit coat off and handed it to the flight attendant. "But I want to make sure things are all right between us. I'm sorry for putting you in that position, James. Had I known you were there, I never would have shown up. That's not who I am."

"I know. It's fine; don't worry."

The phone beside me rang, and I held it against my ear as the captain told me we were getting ready to taxi. I gave him my thanks and hung up.

"Taking off?" Max asked.

"Within the next five minutes."

He opened his briefcase and took out his laptop, setting it on the table in front of him. "How was the meeting with Ralph?"

I stared at James and said, "Tell him."

"It was good."

I laughed, squeezing her foot to urge her to say more. When she didn't, I added, "Don't listen to her. She fucking nailed the audition, and Ralph wants her; he just wants her personal shit cleared up first. Once we get that all figured out, he's going to be calling."

She pressed her other foot against my stomach, like she was tapping me. "You don't know that."

"It's my job to know that."

"Well, since we're far from figuring out my personal shit, I don't see that phone call coming anytime soon."

"Don't tell me that the police aren't doing anything," Max said as the plane started moving toward the runway.

I nodded. "They're out of options. So, if something happens with this case, it's because we found out more information or some asshole in Hollywood opened his mouth."

Max looked at James and said, "It'll happen. I give it two more months before someone spills."

The flight attendant brought Max a scotch, refilled mine, and gave James a new glass of champagne. This was her third drink, and her cheeks were getting flushed.

I fucking loved that color on her.

"How'd your meetings go today?" I asked Max.

"I don't even know where to start," he said.

As he filled me in, neglecting to mention anything about Sophia, I bounced my gaze between him and James. I could tell she wasn't upset with Max. She was just upset in general, and it all had to do with Sophia. That fucking cunt rubbed my girl the wrong way, and I didn't blame her. I knew James just wanted to be done with her and Abel, but that wasn't easy when you worked in the same industry, your paths had the ability to constantly cross, and your agents were business partners.

And, now, there was a chance James could run into Sophia again in the very near future. But, this time, it would be on her turf.

In about a week, The Agency would be celebrating its six-year anniversary, and we were throwing a huge bash in Miami. Sophia was on the guest list. Although she hadn't yet RSVP'd, I had a feeling she'd be there, especially after tonight.

Unless Sophia told us she was coming, I wasn't going to mention any of that to James. Knowing James, she was already feeling the stress about the possibility of seeing her again, and I didn't want that to weigh on her.

The plane started to pick up speed, and I relaxed further into the couch, my arm going under the blanket and landing on James's inner thigh. She made no reaction until my fingers began to trace her jeans, and they continued to move higher until they reached her pussy.

That was when her fucking eyes connected with mine. The need I usually saw in there wasn't as strong, but it would be once I got both hands on her. And that was going to happen the second we reached cruising altitude.

In all the years The Agency had used a private plane, I'd never once fucked on it. I'd never even brought a woman on board unless she was a client.

It was time to change that.

I waited until the flight attendant came back to check on our drinks, knowing that would be a good time to get up.

And, once she left for refills, I said to Max, "You want the back bedroom?"

He looked up from his computer. "Nah, I've got a lot of work to do. It's all yours, buddy."

I leaned into James's ear. "There's a TV in there, so we can finish watching the movie."

She got up from the couch without saying a word and followed me into the bedroom.

I shut the door behind us and immediately grabbed her waist. Lifting her into my arms, I roared, "Kiss me."

As her lips landed on mine, I yanked her tank top over her head and set her on the bed, so I could take off her jeans. I unhooked her bra and slid her panties down her legs. "Crawl to the back of the bed," I ordered.

She turned around and got on all fours, her ass now pointed at me, and she moved toward the other side of the double bed. As she reached the pillows, she looked over her shoulder to watch what I was doing. I was loosening my tie and setting my jacket over the small table. My pants dropped next, and I kicked off my shoes. Before I knelt onto the bed, I let my boxer briefs fall.

From where I stood, I had the most perfect view of her cunt. Those tight, hairless lips ran around the back until the start of her ass.

Fuck, I wanted to be inside of that, too.

"You have no idea how beautiful you are."

Her cheeks were still so red from the champagne, but now, they were several shades deeper.

I fucking loved that I did that to her.

"Come show me," she breathed.

I stared at her mouth, at her pussy, at her ass.

All three were mine.

And I was going to be in all three tonight.

I walked over to the side of the bed and ran my fingers through her hair, turning her and leading her over to me, aiming her mouth to the end of my cock. She spread her lips and took in my crown, swiveling her tongue around it before she bobbed down my shaft.

"*Yesss,*" I hissed.

Damn, she really knew how to suck cock, and she knew how I liked mine sucked.

"Just like that, baby," I said as she tickled my balls at the same time. "Look at me."

Her lids widened as she glanced up. I could see the suction in her cheeks and the way her eyes watered as my tip neared the back of her throat. Every time I hit it, I felt the spit in her mouth thicken, and her nose flared just slightly while she took in air.

"Lick my balls," I demanded.

A popping sound came from her mouth as she freed my dick and lowered to my sack. Gently, her tongue circled one of my balls, and then she surrounded it with her lips. She teased it the same way I would do to her nipple. And, just when she soaked it with plenty of spit, she moved to the other one, her hand sliding up and down my shaft at the same time.

"Fuck," I growled, not wanting to wait a second longer to have her.

I lifted her hand off my dick and moved her onto her back, kneeling between her legs. I pushed them open even further and held her knees while I thrust inside her.

"Brett," she moaned as I drove into her. "Oh my God. That feels so good."

And it did, goddamn it.

She was so wet, so tight, so hot as her cunt squeezed my cock.

I lifted her ass, holding it in the air while I stroked in and out, twisting my hips, making sure to hit the spot she liked.

"*Yesss!*" she shouted.

Her fingers spread over my thighs, her nails digging into my skin, and I knew that meant she was getting close. Hell, I could feel her tightening even more. I could see the way her back was arching. So, I pumped faster, letting her ride out the orgasm with as much speed and pressure as I could give her.

"I'm coming!" she yelled, not giving a fuck if anyone on this plane could hear her.

I sure as hell didn't either.

That was why I pounded into her even harder, so she would scream even louder.

She did, and when she finally calmed, I pulled out and flipped her onto her stomach, moving in behind her. I took some of the wetness from her cunt, and I coated it over my cock, making sure the head was nice and wet. Then, I dipped my face into her ass and gave her my tongue.

She wiggled as I licked, as I dropped wads of spit every time a little bit filled my mouth. And, once it started dripping onto the bed, I pulled back and stroked my dick.

"I can't wait to feel how fucking tight your ass is."

"Brett—"

"I'll go slow."

"Please, like really slow."

I pushed my thumb in first, waiting to feel some resistance, but she didn't give me any. I went in to my knuckle and then slid out before giving her two fingers.

She moved with me.

She fucking moaned with me.

Pulling my fingers out, I aimed my cock at her entrance, and I gently pushed in just an inch.

"You're so big," she breathed.

And I knew she was working through the pain.

I waited several seconds before I gave her any more. Each shift came with a pause, and I reached around and rubbed her clit at the same time. It didn't take more than a minute before I was all the way inside her.

"Jesus fucking Christ, you're tighter than I've ever felt."

Still, I didn't move. I stayed right where I was, and I let her get used to the feeling.

If she didn't loosen at all, I wasn't going to last long, but maybe, for my first time in her ass, she'd prefer that.

I rubbed her clit a little harder, and when her hips began to bounce, I knew she was ready. I slid back so carefully and drove in again.

"*Ahhh,*" she moaned, showing me the preparation had been worth it. "That feels incredible."

It took me a while to work up any speed or power, but I eventually got there, my fingers still on her clit, my other hand holding her gorgeous fucking ass.

The movement of the plane drove me in further. So did the slight grind of her hips as the orgasm began to build within her.

"I'm so close," she cried out.

"Fuck," I panted as the build worked its way through my body.

What she did next surprised the hell out of me.

She put her feet on my thighs and stilled my thrusting, and then she started to fuck me. She went back to the tip before burying my cock, repeating that movement over and over.

"Oh my God!" she yelled, her ass tightening so much that it sucked the cum right out of me.

I took my hand off her clit, and I held her hips as I watched her swallow me. My head went back, my fucking moans vibrating through my chest, and I lost myself.

"James," I groaned.

Each time she slammed onto my cock brought me more pleasure, and I let it pass through me without trying to control it. She knew what she was doing to me, and she knew her ass was holding me so goddamn tight because each hiss that came from my mouth told her.

When the feeling finally released me, I slid back all the way and watched her ass pucker. "Push it out," I told her.

As she stayed on all fours, I watched her ass slightly open, and a bubble of cum dripped from it.

It was the hottest fucking sight.

So hot that I felt my cock start to get hard again.

"Do not move," I ordered.

"Where are you going?"

I reached for my boxers and slid them on. "I'm going to wash you off, and then I'm coming right back to fuck your pussy."

"You're relentless."

"No, James, I just can't get enough of you."

28

JAMES

I SAW Eve sitting on the counter as Brett and I made our way into Max's kitchen.

There was an extra glass of wine right next to her that she handed to me and said, "Cheers, bitch."

"Cheers," I responded. I snaked my arms around her neck, pulling her in for the tightest hug. As I released her, I saw the guys do their kind of hug, and then Brett grabbed a beer out of the fridge.

"I've been told I can't talk about Sophia," Eve said, rolling her eyes so hard. "So, this is me not talking about her." She took a sip of her wine. "Can you believe my fucking boyfriend represents the enemy? Okay, now, I'm really not talking about her."

I looked at Brett and laughed as we'd just had this conversation during our drive over here. He'd told me not to bring up Sophia. I hadn't planned to, but I knew, if Max had told Eve, it would be impossible for her not to mention Sophia.

And I was right.

"Told ya," I said to Brett.

"Eve," Max warned, "you know how I feel about this."

"I know," she said. "I just had to mention it, babe. Now, it's out of my system, and we can move on."

"You sure you're done?" he asked her.

She held her glass to her lips again and took a large gulp. "Mmhmm."

Eve had just gotten into town this morning and come straight to Max's place where she'd be for the next week. I knew I'd see her the whole time she was here, so I wasn't bummed that she was staying with him. Besides, I was basically living at Brett's anyway. I hadn't moved any of my things in, but given that I only lived a few floors down, it wasn't hard to pop by my place for a change of clothes.

Since her first visit, she'd been shipping me outfits to wear for all my events. Now that she was in Miami, she could stock me up. My calendar was getting extremely busy, and I really needed something amazing to wear to The Agency's sixth-anniversary party that was going to be in a few days. Max had asked Eve to be his date, which was another reason she had flown in.

As for Brett and me, no one at the party would know we were together. They couldn't. It wasn't the right time for that. If the media found out we were dating, they'd say the most awful things about me. So, like any other night we were out in public, Brett and I would just be agent and actress.

Regardless, I wanted to look my best for him.

I went over to the island and rested my elbows on top of it. "What are you making?" I asked Max.

"It's always Italian when Max cooks," Brett said.

"And it's delicious," Eve added.

She'd told me he had cooked for her during the time he stayed with her in LA.

"We've got about five minutes until it's ready," Max said. "How about you take James out back, so Brett and I can talk a little business?"

Eve slid off the counter. She looped her arm through mine and brought me out the sliding glass door. There was a massive patio with a fireplace and several seating areas. His pool was a giant rectangle where the water ran off the edge, and directly beyond it was the ocean.

It was the most beautiful view.

Eve was right next to me as I stood on the bank, looking at the houses across the way and at the open water. A few boats were passing through, and some of the people waved.

"It's so peaceful here," I said.

"You have no idea. I went swimming today and fell asleep in the pool." She tugged down the shoulder of her shirt to show me how red she was. "You know this is what we're going to be doing every day I'm here, so get ready for some major relaxation."

I smiled at her from the corner of my eye. "Don't think you're getting off from styling me. I need tons of new stuff."

"I have fifteen outfits for you upstairs, and another ten are getting delivered tomorrow. We'll have a fashion show when you come over for lunch."

"You got all of that already?"

She nodded and did a little dance in her heels. "Wait until you see the dress I picked out for you for The Agency party. Brett is going to *diiie* when he sees you. We're not going to have him approve it; you're just going to show up, wearing it, and he's going to take you in the restroom and fuck your brains out."

"He'll be pissed if he doesn't see the dress first."

"Trust me, he's going to have plenty of other things on his mind, so he won't even remember that he hasn't approved it."

I took a drink from my wine. "Has the party been stressful to plan?"

I was surprised I didn't know what Eve was talking about, and I wondered what else was on his mind. Brett didn't talk business a lot, mostly because any communication with his clients was confidential. But he did mention things about The Agency in general, like how well his team was producing and how quickly they were growing and how they needed to hire more support staff.

"The guys aren't planning the party. Some big-time Miami party planner is doing all the work. I'm talking about the guest list."

"What do you mean?"

She turned toward me and stared into my eyes, searching them like she was looking for something. And then, almost immediately, an expression of shock covered her face. "Oh my God, you don't know."

"Know what?"

"Brett is going to murder me."

"Why?"

"No, Brett won't have a chance to murder me because Max is going to kill me first."

I set my wine on the ground and put my hands on her shoulders to stop her from moving. "What the hell are you talking about?"

She shook her head, her mouth finally opening. "I don't know how to tell you this, so I'm just going to come out and say it."

"Okay."

"James, I'm so sorry."

I held her tighter. "Eve, you're dragging this out, and it's making me nervous."

"That's because I have to tell you something I really don't want to, and I wanted to hurt someone when I found out myself."

"Say it already."

"Sophia and Abel are coming to the party."

She'd blurted it out so fast, I wasn't sure I'd heard her correctly.

"What?"

"Yeah, I know. And, now, you know why I was so pissed when I found out. I mean, it's one thing to represent the enemy. But to invite her to a party that you're going to be at? That's just shitty. He told me they couldn't *not* invite her. It would be crappy from a professional standpoint, but..."

I stopped listening to what she was saying and tried to process what it would feel like when I saw Abel and Sophia in Miami.

Florida had become my safe place. It was where I could be myself and not hide. It was where I felt most comfortable, and now, that was going to be taken away from me.

By two people who had hurt me so much.

"I think I'm going to be sick."

"No, you're not," she said, putting her arm around my shoulders and leading me toward one of the couches on the other side of the patio. When we reached it, she sat us both in the middle. "Listen to me, you're going to put on the sexy dress I got for you, and you're going to walk into that party like you're the hottest, most successful actress in the room. No matter how those two dickheads look, no matter what they say to you, no matter how much you hate them, you're not going to let them get to you." I tried to say something, but she cut me off, "Remember, if you show them how much they affect you, then they win. We will not let that happen."

"I'm definitely going to be sick."

"You're already letting them win, James."

I faced her, crossing my legs over the cushions, rubbing my hands on my knees to get rid of the sweat. "Eve, you have no idea how hard it was to see Sophia at that restaurant in LA."

"Because of Abel?"

"No. It's not even about him. I don't care that she has him. I'm not in love with him anymore. It's all the things she said to me that day in their house. She made me feel like I was the worst person in the world, and I can't seem to let that go."

She grabbed my hand and held it between hers. "What can I do?"

"Maybe I just won't go."

"You're going. Don't even say that."

"Ladies," Max said from the doorway, "dinner is ready."

Eve's eyes moved from him to me. "Fuck, you're going to say something, aren't you?" She put her other hand on my cheek. "You can't hide it. It's all over your face."

"I'll try not to bring it up."

"It's okay; you're allowed to scream at him. He should have told you, so I don't feel bad for spilling the beans."

I'd been so caught up in the news, I hadn't even considered Brett's involvement in all of this. He had a horrible habit of keeping things from me. He'd been doing it since the day I met him, and it had only gotten worse.

"Come on," she said, helping me stand and leading me back inside.

The guys were in the kitchen, filling their arms with dishes and carrying them into the dining room. On the table, there was wine in the glasses and a basket of bread in the middle along with large plates of pasta and meatballs, what looked like chicken Parmesan, and something else with eggplant.

It smelled good, but I didn't think I could put a bite of it into my mouth.

Eve brought me over to the table. I lifted one of the glasses, held it to my lips, and guzzled until it was empty.

When I pulled it away from my mouth, I felt Brett's stare on me.

And Eve's.

And Max's.

Brett then broke contact to look at Eve before he came back to me. "Thirsty?"

I reached for the bottle and refilled my glass halfway, gazing at the dark red liquid, not sure if I could even take another sip. Eventually, I glanced up. With the three of them still looking at me, I said, "You should have told me."

"Jesus, Brett," Max said. "I hope she's not talking about what I think she is. And I hope to hell you weren't the one who told her, Eve."

"I thought Brett had told her," she snapped.

Brett said nothing. He just continued to stare at me.

"You've done this to me too many times." My voice was so quiet. I couldn't yell. I couldn't get mad. I was too hurt for that.

"James, that's not fucking true," Brett said. "I've only done it once before, and that was when I first met you. There was a reason I didn't tell you I was an agent, and you know what that reason is. Don't compare that to this, goddamn it."

He waited for me to comment. I didn't.

"I promise, I wouldn't have let you walk into that party without you knowing who was going to be there."

"That doesn't make it okay."

He walked over to me and put his hand in the back of my hair, tightly holding my head. "No, it doesn't. I know it was wrong to keep it from you. But I didn't want to hurt you, and I knew that was what this news would do."

"Brett..."

He held me with even more power. "I'm just as fucking pissed as you are. The last thing I want is that cunt at my party. She's going to ruin my time. I'd like to call her myself and tell her not to come, but I can't, and you know why."

"Max, everyone in this room hates you right now," Eve said.

"Jesus Christ," Max said. He was the only one sitting, the only one with food on his plate, the only one who was eating. When he realized we were all looking at him, he put his fork down. "When are you all going to accept that Sophia is my client? I'm not uninviting her. I'm not asking her to leave early. I'm not saying a goddamn word to her about any of this. You're both adults, and you'll have to figure out a way to play nice, for the sake of The Agency."

My stare moved back to Brett as he said, "I want to make this better."

I shook my head. "You can't."

I pulled his hand off me and walked over to my seat, putting a few noodles on my plate, knowing I'd have the hardest time even getting those down.

Sophia was going to come, and there was nothing anyone in this room could do about it. I could scream at Brett, I could start a fight, I could spend the night at my place tonight instead of his. But it wouldn't solve anything.

I just had to get through this party.

And, somehow, I would.

29

BRETT

FOR TONIGHT'S PARTY, The Agency had rented out the patio and pool deck at one of the most exclusive hotels on South Beach. We'd told the party planner we wanted the vibe to be extremely upscale and sexy, and she'd certainly delivered. We needed our clients to feel confident in their choice of representation and that we'd never spare any expense when it came to their best interests. From the way everyone was laughing and smiling, I'd say our half-a-million-dollar budget had accomplished our goal.

The only thing missing was James.

She and Eve had been taking their sweet time in arriving, and I knew that had to do with Abel and Sophia being on the guest list.

Since James had found out they were attending, she hadn't been acting like herself. I knew that was her anxiety kicking in, the same way I knew, at some point, she'd try to get out of coming. And she had this morning after I got out of the shower. She'd been sitting at the end of my bed, a robe wrapped around her, looking at me with the most pleading eyes. I'd told her she could do whatever made her comfortable but that I hoped, for me, she'd be there.

I'd worked so fucking hard for this company. I just wanted to share the success with her tonight even if that meant I couldn't touch her. That part would have to wait until I got her home where I would live inside her pussy until she was too sore to take any more.

I tried to get that thought out of my head as I made my way around the pool deck, seeing Jack and Max and Scarlett doing the same, shaking hands with our clients, talking about upcoming deals and negotiations, hearing buzz about the industry. Some of the biggest names in sports, movies, and music were here tonight, and they all wanted in on the next best thing.

We would get them that.

And, in the morning, we would take everything we had learned tonight, and we'd meet with our teams. We'd separate rumors from fact, and we'd come up with a plan of how we were going to go after those contracts.

This party wasn't just a celebration. It was the start of another wave of business, and millions of dollars would be earned on both sides of these deals.

This was why we threw an annual bash.

And this was why it had to go perfectly because the last fucking thing any of us needed was an outburst of any kind.

As I stepped away from one of Jack's athletes, I headed around the side bar toward the other end of the patio. I made it about halfway before Scarlett stopped me and said, "She's here."

I knew she was talking about James because Sophia and Abel had already been here for a while.

"Is she all right?"

Scarlett knew James and I were together. Jack did also. I'd felt it was important that my partners were kept informed, just in case the media somehow got tipped off and outed us.

"She looks nervous, even with Eve trying to calm her," Scarlett said. "I don't think she plans on drinking, but it wouldn't be a bad idea if she had just one to take the edge off. I wouldn't suggest more than that."

"That's a good idea." I called over the closest waiter and said to him, "Would you mind bringing me a glass of champagne?"

"No problem," he replied.

"I got a chance to talk to Eve this afternoon," Scarlett said once we were alone again. "She's going to keep an eye on Abel and Sophia to keep them and James on separate sides of the room. And I briefed the security team, too, just to make them aware of it. You know I never like to be too safe."

"If Sophia says a fucking word to James, we won't need security because I'll be kicking her ass out myself. I don't give a shit if she's Max's client; I won't tolerate her bullshit."

"Max doesn't seem worried at all."

I glanced to my right and saw Abel on a chair, sitting around the fire pit, with Sophia on his lap. They had drinks in their hands and were talking to several of Max's other clients.

"That's because Max doesn't know how much of a bitch that cunt can be or the things Sophia has said to James in the past." The waiter returned with James's drink, and I gripped her glass and mine in both hands. "Where is she?"

"When I saw her last, she was standing with Eve near the entrance."

"I need to go see her. I'll talk to you in a little while," I said, and I made my way toward the front.

Every few feet, I got stopped by either a client or a team member. I told each of them I'd be back to chat and continued heading toward the entrance. Rounding the corner of the last bar, I walked up the steps that separated the upper section of the pool deck from the main level, and I saw her immediately.

It didn't matter that only her profile faced me.

I would have spotted that body anywhere, and my cock immediately responded to it.

Dressed in the palest yellow two-piece, the tank top she had on was cut low over her chest and ended right below her tits. Her stomach was bare and revealed. Then, the skirt started right above her belly button where it tightly wrapped across her ass and thighs and ended at her ankles.

I hadn't been shown this outfit.

She'd hear about that tomorrow.

Right now, I couldn't get over how fucking hot she looked.

And how I was going to take those two pieces off with my goddamn teeth.

Shaking my head, moving that fantasy to the side, I joined the two of them and handed James the champagne. "Scarlett thought you could use this."

Her gaze shot all over me. "Hi."

Scarlett was right; James was nervous as fuck. When she put her lips around the glass, I saw it shake before the champagne reached her mouth.

"Drink it slow," I told her.

She swallowed once and pulled it away.

"You look gorgeous."

I held my tumbler with both hands, so I wouldn't be tempted to touch her. It was painful that I couldn't. That I wasn't able to lean into her neck and take in her pear scent. That I couldn't move that small piece of hair that was stuck to her glossy lips. That I couldn't tell her how gorgeous she was while I was kissing her.

"Thank you." She blushed, and this time, I knew it wasn't from the champagne.

"Are you okay?" I asked and then looked at Eve, but her eyes were on James.

"I'm here, and I'll stay as long as you want me to."

She was such a goddamn pleaser. That was something I liked about her. What I didn't like was that she wasn't being honest with me, and I needed an answer before I could go anywhere.

"Are you okay, James?" My voice was quiet but demanding.

Her eyes shifted to the glass for several seconds before they came back to me. "I will be."

"I'll make sure of it," Eve said.

"Do you need anything?"

She shook her head. "It's your party; you need to go talk to everyone and have fun. I'll see you later."

I fucking hated that I had to walk away and not take her back to my place where she wouldn't have to see those two bastards. But she was right; I needed to work the room, and it would take me most of the night to speak to everyone here.

"If you need anything, you text me. My phone is right in my pocket, and I'll feel it vibrate."

"She'll be fine," Eve said.

James said nothing. She just stared at me until I turned around.

I knew Eve had meant every word she said, and she would take care of her. Those girls would do anything for each other. But it wasn't the same as having James next to me where I could make sure nothing happened.

It was going to be a long fucking night.

30

JAMES

BRETT THOUGHT the reason I was such a mess was because Abel and Sophia were attending the party. He was right, but that wasn't the whole reason. The day after Eve had arrived, while we'd been swimming in Max's pool, I'd decided tonight was when I would confront the two of them about Calvin and see if they knew anything about him.

They were the only ones I hadn't asked. And, because I knew Abel so well, I'd know if he was lying, so face-to-face was the only way to do it.

While Eve and I had been getting ready, she'd tried to talk me out of it. She knew Scarlett would be angry since Eve had promised to keep me away from them. She'd promised Max. And she'd promised Brett several times that she'd take care of me, and part of that meant keeping me separated from them.

I knew what everyone wanted.

But this wasn't about them. This was about me getting my career back. We weren't any closer to identifying Calvin, and if there was something Abel or Sophia remembered, maybe there was a chance the police could find him.

All I wanted was to clear my name.

So, while Eve and I had been hanging out on the top section of the patio deck, I'd had her constantly checking out Abel and Sophia's location. I didn't want to approach them when a lot of people were around. I wanted to wait until they were alone.

Less than an hour after Brett left us, the opportunity came.

They were standing on the far side of the pool, closest to the beach, leaning into a railing that overlooked the ocean. It appeared to be a quieter area, and there weren't many people near them.

"Let's go," I told her, and I scanned all the different paths I could take that would bring us there.

"Are you sure?"

"No, I'm definitely not sure, but I have to do this, or I'll regret it."

"Brett is going to fucking kill me, so can we make sure he doesn't see you guys talking? That means, no yelling and no fists being thrown."

"I'm not going to punch the girl."

"I was talking about me. So, don't say anything to provoke her; that way, I won't have to knock her out."

Instead of responding, I grabbed her hand, and we made our way down the stairs and toward the side of the pool, so I wouldn't have to walk through the middle.

Since I'd arrived, Eve and I had stayed glued in our spot near the entrance. Before the video had been leaked, I would have walked around the room, introduced myself, and chatted with everyone I knew. But, now, all I thought about was that the people here had seen me naked. And that was enough to keep me planted away from the crowd.

Staying to the side, where hardly anyone was standing, I took us straight toward the back and up the few short steps until we were on the upper balcony and just a few feet from them.

Only a few months ago, I would have wanted to tell Abel how much I loved him, hoping he would say it in return. I would have wanted to know why he'd chosen her over me.

Not now.

As I looked at his back, at the two of them cuddling with his arms around her, I felt no love for him. In its place, I felt anger at the way he had hurt me. At the way he had treated me. I felt disgust over his cheating.

The betrayal I felt weighed so much more than any of the good times we'd shared.

Eve squeezed my hand before I took another step and mouthed, *Are you sure?*

I nodded and continued walking until I stood at the railing next to Sophia. "Can I talk to you?"

Her head snapped in my direction, and she gave me the same look as when she had seen me at the restaurant in LA. "What the fuck do you want?"

Slowly, my stare moved to Abel. This was the first time I'd seen him in person since the last party we were both at. It was the first time I'd felt his eyes on me. The first time I'd looked at his face, the one I'd kissed so many times and loved on and whispered all my goals and fears to.

And this was the first time I saw him for who he really was— the asshole who had lied and cheated and not given a shit about me.

I'd known the second Brett touched me outside the ladies' room at the bar that he was the man I was supposed to be with.

I knew that even more now.

Abel was my past, and I felt nothing for him. All I wanted was to ask him a question, and then I never wanted to speak to him again.

"James," he said softly.

It was just one word, but it was a powerful one. And it had been spoken right at me with what sounded like a little sympathy.

It was far too late for that.

After a quick glance at Eve, I shifted on my feet and moved my gaze to Sophia. "I just need to ask you both something. Then, I'll leave you alone."

"Why don't you turn around and leave us alone now?" Sophia said.

"Why don't you relax?" Eve spit back at her.

"Who the fuck are you?" Sophia snarled. "The director of the porn video or the girl who fixed James's makeup when she was done banging him?"

"Listen, you fucking bitch—"

Abel interrupted Eve by saying, "Sophia, just let her speak."

I took a deep breath, thinking of how I should word this. I had one chance, and if I messed it up, Sophia wasn't going to give me another.

"There was a guy I hung out with at that party," I started with. "We were together most of the afternoon and into the night. A few times, we passed where you guys were sitting."

"What's the point?" Sophia hissed.

"Do you remember him? Or what he looks like?"

"No," Sophia said. "I barely remember you being at that party."

That was a lie.

Every time my eyes had caught hers, she'd made sure to lay on the PDA extra thick. She'd definitely seen me; she just wouldn't give me the satisfaction of knowing it.

"He had messy brown hair," I added. "An extra-big smile. Larger teeth in the front. Some freckles under his eyes. He was about the same height as you, Abel."

"You want me to recall someone who had large teeth? Is this some kind of joke?"

"No, it's not a joke," I said. "I need to know if you saw him there."

"Big teeth doesn't sound familiar," she said, laughing.

I looked at Abel. "How about you?"

It appeared as though he was thinking about my question, his face softening the more he stared at me.

Sophia turned toward him and said, "Come on, babe. Let's go. This is ridiculous."

His eyes stayed on me, and eventually, he shook his head.

"Are you sure, Abel?"

I just needed to hear his voice. I needed to see the way his eyes changed when he gave me an answer. I needed to see his expression when his mouth opened.

But he gave me none of that. He just nodded, and Sophia grabbed his hand. Then, the two of them walked away.

"She's a real piece of work," Eve said. "He's going to get sick of that quickly. My God, I can't believe he hasn't already. Her voice makes me want to stab my ears."

I needed a second away from this party to reset my thoughts before I returned to the perch we'd been standing on for most of the night.

"I'm going to run to the restroom," I told her. "I'll meet you back where we were before in a couple of minutes."

"I'll go with you."

I put my hand on her bare shoulder. "I'll be fine. Don't worry. Just wait for me on the upper patio."

She nodded, and I went inside the hotel, weaving through the short hallway and into the ladies' room where I locked myself in a stall. I took out my phone and scrolled through my messages just to get my mind off the last few minutes.

It didn't work.

All I could see was the hatred on Sophia's face. I had no idea why she disliked me so much. The only thing that made sense was that she felt threatened by me. I didn't know why since she clearly had more of Abel than I had. She had to be an extremely insecure person, obviously worried that Abel would cheat like he'd done when he was with me.

Those two assholes deserve each other.

But, now, what really sucked, besides that I'd had to go to my enemies for help, was that I still wasn't any closer to finding out who Calvin was, and I had no one else to turn to.

Knowing I wouldn't come up with any answers in here, I left the stall and went over to the sink to wash my hands. I barely had the water turned on when I heard the restroom door open. Quickly looking over my shoulder, I saw Sophia walk in and reach behind herself to twist the lock.

"We need to talk," she said.

My stomach began to churn, my hands shaking so badly that I had to wrap them around my body. "What do you want?"

"I want you to leave Abel alone." She took a couple more steps, and now, she was only a few feet away. "I've asked you this repeatedly, but you're not a very good listener, are you, James?"

"I have left him alone."

"What do you call tonight then? Coming up to us at a party to ask us the most pathetic question, which was just an excuse to talk to him. God, you're so desperate."

"You have it all wrong."

"Abel is fucking disgusted that you filmed a sex tape and showed your pussy to the entire world. You repulse him. He wants nothing to do with you, and he doesn't want to talk to you. So, what is it going to take to get you to realize that? Because I feel like I've tried everything. I've warned you, and I've threatened you, and you still haven't listened to me."

"Abel means nothing to me."

She laughed, and it was the most obnoxious sound. "Do you expect me to believe that? I know you're obsessed with him."

She was goading me. Fighting back was what she wanted. And it was taking everything I had not to tell her about Brett. But she was really starting to test me.

"I think you're the one who's obsessed with him." I went to step around her, and she mirrored my movement. "We're finished here."

"Oh no, we're not, honey. I asked you what it was going to take. I want a fucking answer."

The sickness in my stomach was gone. Now, there was just anger, and it was running through my whole body.

"I'm telling you, I'm done," I demanded.

"I don't believe you."

I heard someone at the restroom door. They were trying to pull it open, but because of the lock, it wouldn't budge.

"Believe me," I said, "I won't be wasting my time talking to either of you. I've moved on, Sophia. You really need to, too. Dwelling on the past makes you look like a psycho, jealous girlfriend."

"Fiancée."

"Yikes," I said. "That's even worse."

"Open this door right now, or I'll call security," I heard Eve say.

Eve is the person at the door?

She's come to check on me.

God, I love her.

"Go ahead," Sophia muttered. "Run off to your porn director. I'm done with you anyway." She moved over to the counter and started opening her clutch, like she was going to grab a lipstick.

I rushed around her and met Eve outside in the hallway.

"Why the hell was the door locked?" she asked when I clung my arm around hers.

"Sophia locked it."

"She's in there?" She stopped and turned, as though she was going to go into the restroom. "I'll kill that bitch."

"Eve, no." I squeezed her hand. "That's what she wants, and I'm done pleasing her."

She looked at me with her teeth clenched. "Then, we're going to go tell Brett what happened because her ass needs to be kicked out."

Oh, boy.

If this was the way Eve was reacting, I could only imagine how Brett was going to respond when I told him Sophia had locked me in the restroom.

The problem was, maybe I had asked for it by confronting them at the party.

Unfortunately, that was something I'd have to tell him, too.

31

BRETT

MAX, Eve, James, and I were on the top floor of the hotel in a suite that the party planner had reserved for the night. She'd wanted us to have it in case we needed a break or to change our clothes or hold a private meeting.

I sure as fuck hadn't planned on using it, so my girlfriend and her best friend could tell me what had just gone down with Abel and Sophia after promising they wouldn't go anywhere near them.

I looked at Max, my anger boiling, as James told me she'd gotten locked in the restroom and the things Sophia had said to her while they were in there. Eve picked up the rest of the story from the moment James had left the restroom until she found us on the pool deck. That was when I'd handed Eve a room key and told her I was going to find Max and that we would meet them in the suite.

"Jesus Christ," Max groaned as soon as Eve was finished. He leaned against the back of the couch, his arms crossed, his stare on the ground. "This is what I was afraid of and why I didn't want either of you to go anywhere near them. You poked the bear, and Sophia exploded."

What the hell did he just say?

"I can't believe what I'm hearing right now," I snapped at him. "I fucking know you didn't just stick up for that cunt."

"Agreed," Eve said, looking like she was about to tackle him.

"You girls had no right to talk to them."

Before I had a chance to yell at Max, James chimed in with, "I had every right."

The girls were sitting on the couch across from us. James was on the edge of it, fidgeting nonstop.

"The detective asked me to reach out to everyone at the party that night to see if they knew Calvin. The two of them were there, so I had to say something. You would have done the same if you were in my situation."

"I would have called them," Max said.

"Don't you think I would have done that, too, if I thought they would answer my call? But let's be real; we both know Sophia would never do that. I had one chance to confront them, and I took it."

Max shook his head, but he knew she was right.

Hell, I wasn't fucking happy that she'd confronted them either, but she was taking her situation by the balls, and she was trying to make it better. Given their past, it had taken some nerve for her to go up to them. And, based on how anxious she'd been over the last few days, I had a feeling it was something she'd been debating.

"Do you think you'll be able to go back down there and ignore them? Because, if you return to the party, that's what I need you to do," Max said to the both of them.

"Wait one fucking second," I snapped at Max. "You want James to go down to the party and forget about it, like nothing happened? I don't think so."

"What are you suggesting, Brett?"

I didn't care if he was my best friend. He was also my business partner, and when shit happened between clients, our friendship was no longer on the table. We would hash this out the same way we would if we were negotiating a deal.

"Sophia needs to go. I want her ass sent home immediately, and I want her contract terminated as of tomorrow morning. She needs to find a new company to represent her."

"You're unbelievable, you know that?" Max said. He walked over to the windows and turned around, so his back was resting against the glass. "You really think that locking a restroom door warrants a termination of her fucking contract? That's the same thing we chastised the agents in LA for doing. It's petty, it's childish, and it's not who we are."

"This is different," I growled.

"Why? Because James is your girlfriend? Because, if this were any other client, we wouldn't be up here, having this conversation. We would have told security to calm them down, and we wouldn't have given it another thought. But, now, we're up here, talking about a client I make a lot of money off of and the beef she has with your girlfriend. And none of it is relevant to The Agency. I told you I wouldn't get involved, and I meant it."

"That's it?" I roared. "That's all you have to say about this?"

He stopped and looked at me. "Brett, I understand where you're coming from, and I know this hits you personally, so I'm excusing your reaction, but I don't think Sophia did anything wrong. James made the first move, and Sophia made the last one. Sounds like they're pretty even to me."

Max was right. I was treating this situation differently because James was my girlfriend.

I didn't give a fuck.

Sophia had threatened my girl, and I wasn't going to tolerate it.

"Get rid of her, Max."

He continued walking to the door and turned around as he gripped the handle. "We'll have a meeting with Jack and Scarlett about it on Monday and get them to weigh in. In the meantime, Sophia stays." He looked at James. "I wish this hadn't happened, and I'm sorry it got to this. I hope you understand where I'm coming from."

He gave James a chance to respond, and she said nothing, so he walked out.

"I'm going to murder him," Eve said.

I agreed, but I didn't respond, and neither did James.

Several seconds of silence passed before I said, "I'll figure it out. I'll talk to security and—"

"No, Brett." James stood and moved closer to me. "I didn't tell you what had happened to get her kicked out. I told you because Eve had forced me to." She glanced at her best friend, who looked like she was about to become unhinged. "Max is in a shitty situation, and as much as I hate Sophia, I get where he's coming from. We all don't need to hold this against him. From a business standpoint, he's doing the right thing."

"You're more understanding than me," I said.

"And me," Eve replied.

"Listen to me, I need you to go back down there and finish the party. I'm going to head home."

I didn't want her to fucking leave, especially because of that cunt. But I wouldn't put her in a situation where she could be threatened again, and kicking out her enemy after my disagreement with Max wasn't a smart move.

I took my phone out of my pocket, and I sent a message to the front desk of our building. When I finished, I said, "I want you to go to my condo, not yours. Whoever is working the door will take you to my elevator and make sure you get in." I typed another text, this one to her driver. He replied instantly. "The SUV is downstairs, waiting for you."

I closed the distance between James and me, and I pressed my lips against hers. She tasted of champagne and pears, and I wanted to lick it right off her tongue. But, after a short kiss, I pulled away, knowing that, if I didn't stop, I never would.

"Give me a few minutes to get downstairs," I told her. Then, I looked at Eve. "I want you to walk James straight to the lobby and out the front. No stops. Make sure she gets in that car safely, and report back to me that everything went all right."

They both nodded.

I walked toward the door, turning around right before I reached it. My eyes scanned her body one last time, and I knew exactly what I wanted. "When I get home, you'd better still be wearing that dress." I didn't wait for her to respond before I went into the hallway and got in the elevator.

32

BRETT

TWO WEEKS HAD PASSED since the party, and Sophia Sully was still a client of The Agency. Like Max had suggested, we had met with Jack and Scarlett the Monday after and discussed everything that had happened between the girls. My partners were in agreement with Max. They didn't believe the confrontation had anything to do with the company, so there was no reason to end her contract.

That had made me fucking furious.

It had taken some time for me to cool down, but eventually, I understood where they were coming from. I just wasn't happy about it.

And James wasn't pleased that she'd gotten nowhere by asking them if they knew who Calvin was. So, to try to get her mind off things, I had my assistant book us a yacht that would take us to Key West for a long weekend. James had never been before, and it was just what she needed.

Key West was nothing like Miami.

It wasn't fancy, and it certainly wasn't flashy. It wasn't known for its beaches or clubs or even their hotels. Most of the places on the island were a bit of a shithole, which was why we stayed on the boat. But it was a place where James could wear flip-flops and not bother with makeup and dance to the music playing in the street and watch the most incredible sunsets.

And that was what we did for two straight days.

Now, it was our last night here before we'd be cruising back to Miami in the morning, and the staff was clearing our plates after they served us dinner on the top deck.

One of them refilled James's champagne, and then she topped off my scotch and said, "Can I bring you some dessert?"

I looked at James. She was eating the strawberry that had hung over the rim of her glass, her lips wide, taking in the tip, just like she would do to my cock.

She was wearing a low-cut dress and no bra, and her nipples were hard from the breeze. Because I'd seen her get ready after her shower, I knew she didn't have any panties on underneath.

The only dessert I wanted was to feast on her cunt.

"I think we're all right for now," I told her.

She nodded. "Once we're finished tidying up, we'll be out of your hair."

That was a polite way of saying they'd stay off this deck and give us some privacy.

And that was what I wanted.

Once the plates were gone, James slid around the horseshoe-shaped bench until she was right next to me. I put my arm around her shoulders and pulled her into my chest, kissing the top of her head. She smelled so fucking good.

"I think I'm going to sign up for a business class at the University of Miami."

Surprised by her news, I leaned back, so I could see her face. "You're serious?"

She glanced up. "It's online, so I won't have to go to the school and draw all this attention to myself."

"Where did this decision come from?"

She sat up but stayed facing me. "Since middle school, I've been taking classes online, and that's how I got my high school diploma. Technically, I should have started college last fall, and I probably would have majored in business. My accountant and financial adviser manage my money and investments, but I'd like to take a more active role, maybe find some businesses to partner up with. I need more knowledge, and I think the college courses will help with that." Her voice softened. "I certainly have the time now to do it, and I know how happy it would have made my parents."

So often, I forgot that she was only eighteen. That she should have just walked across the stage to receive her diploma, like I'd done with my buddies. That she should be at keg parties and eating grilled cheeses from the cafeteria. That she should have a lack of closet space in a small-ass dorm room.

But James didn't have any of that.

And, still, she was a millionaire.

I loved that money fueled her to want to learn more and to want to have control over her future.

That wasn't a decision most eighteen-year-olds would make.

"Why the University of Miami?"

She shrugged, a smile growing across her face. "I like it here." She glanced around at the scenery beyond the boat. Because it was after sunset, the only light was at the top of the yacht, and it made a path of silver that went straight across the water, almost all the way to the shore. "It's pretty."

I held back a curl that threatened to fall into her face and cupped her cheek. "You're full of shit."

She laughed. "I want to stay to be close to you."

"You know I'm not giving up. My goal is to have you on a movie set within the next three months. I'm fighting like hell for you."

"I know. I want that, too. But that doesn't mean I can't take a class at the same time I'm filming or make Miami my home base instead of LA."

Fuck, I wanted that.

But I wanted it for the right reason.

"James, listen to me, I don't want you to have any regrets. I don't want you to give up anything because of me. I don't want to hold you back. So, I need to know you're doing this for you and not for me."

She said nothing for several breaths. She just stared out toward the water, and I watched the emotion start to fill her face.

"I've learned a lot since Abel. Even more since Calvin." She paused to put her hand on top of mine. "I'm not afraid to go after what I want, Brett. I proved that at your party. And, now, more than ever, I think before I act. I've been thinking about this for weeks."

"If that's what you want, then you're going to give up your apartment and move in with me."

"Really? You're okay with that?"

"You're living with me now anyway. The only things missing are your clothes, and I'm sure I can find a spot for them."

She ran her other hand over the side of my beard. "I want that."

"Me, too."

I lifted my arm off her shoulders and gripped the back of her head, pushing her closer to me. When my lips were right in front of hers, I stopped. "You're mine."

"Yes."

Then, I lifted the bottom of her dress, my fingers crawling underneath it and going higher until they reached her cunt. No panties, just like I'd thought, but two perfect lips and a sexy fucking clit instead. "All of you."

"Yes."

I circled her entrance, her wetness soaking my fingers until two of them slipped in.

"*Ahhh,*" she hissed, her eyes locking with my stare. "And you're all mine."

I devoured her mouth as soon as the words had left it, never hearing her speak something so hot before.

While we'd been eating dinner, I'd scouted places on the top deck where it would be safe to fuck. I needed a spot that wasn't in the light, that would hide her body once I took off her dress. Somewhere that couldn't be seen if another boat drove by or if someone was looking at us from the shore. I'd found a small section in the front that was exactly what I needed. It had a round couch and an awning over the top that covered both sides. And, because it was so dark in that area, the only thing anyone would see was my back.

Before I lost all self-control and stripped her naked right here, I decided it was time to move her.

I slowly slid out of her pussy, and while I stood, I stuck those same fingers into my mouth, groaning as I got a taste of her.

"You're so dirty," she said.

"You're so fucking delicious."

I reached for her waist and lifted her into the air, carrying her to the front of the deck where I set her on the couch.

"Isn't this just the perfect spot?" she said, stretching her legs across the cushions, almost positioning herself in a split. "Knowing you, you planned this."

"Not planned," I said as I knelt in front of her. "But found." I lifted her dress and dived my face underneath it, going straight for her clit.

"Brett," she moaned.

Her hand went to the top of my head, and she yanked my hair as I ate her cunt. I licked up and down, sucking every few seconds, flicking during the rest, my fingers driving into her. She bent her knees, her toes curling around the edge. I could tell she was trying to be quiet, but her gentle moans and her breathing told me she was getting close.

"Just like that," she said, her hips grinding, causing her pussy to rock back and forth over my mouth.

I licked harder and faster and finger-fucked her all the way up to my knuckles. Within a few seconds, she was unraveling, her stomach trembling. Once I knew the orgasm had worked through her body, I pulled her dress over her head and slipped my shirt off, dropping my shorts before I got on my knees again.

"Fuck me," she demanded.

I loved that mouth.

I especially loved it when it said things like that.

I moved her legs apart, placing her thighs on the cushions, and pulled her toward the edge where I thrust straight into her pussy.

"My God," she groaned, my sound matching hers.

I reached around and held her ass, cupping the back of her head with my other hand, and I ground my fucking cock into that tight, wet cunt.

"James," I growled, my hand now running over her tit and down her navel and across her thigh and back up to her neck.

She was so fucking young.

She had the most unbelievable body.

The tightest cunt.

A perfect ass.

A face that couldn't be more gorgeous.

And all of it was mine.

I pounded into her, rubbing her clit at the same time. Just as the build began to clench my balls, she wrapped her arms around my neck and put her lips on mine, and we both moaned.

Knowing she was only seconds away, I brushed her clit even harder and tilted my hips forward to reach that spot she liked.

"Brett," she cried out, her head leaning back, her tits begging for my teeth.

I took one into my mouth and sucked it while I pumped, cum shooting out with every plunge.

"God, you're incredible." She grabbed my face and held it close as the both of us tried to catch our breaths.

I kissed her hard, and when we calmed down and our movements stilled, I said, "You rent your house in LA, don't you?"

"Yes."

"Why don't we fly there at the end of this week, get all your shit packed up, and move you into my place? No reason to keep that lease if you're making Miami home."

Even though it was dark, I could still see her smile.

"I love that idea."

33

JAMES

"WILL YOU BRING ME SOME COFFEE?" I shouted to Brett from the bed while I heard him moving around in the kitchen.

Even on days we could sleep in, he still got up so early. Usually, he'd try dragging me to the gym in our building, but that was after he gave me a workout at home.

I never had to beg.

That man wanted sex all the time, especially since I'd moved in.

It was a little over a month ago when I'd given up the lease of my LA rental and had all my things shipped to Florida. Brett and I had met the moving company at my place, and I'd told them what I wanted to keep and the items that were being donated.

There wasn't any room to put my clothes in the master closet, so I'd chosen to put them in one of the guest rooms. The size of the space was perfect; it just had no organization. So, the day after my stuff had arrived, Brett had had a decorator meet me at the condo to design a new closet. It had taken three weeks to build, and then Eve had flown in a few days ago to fill the sections with even more clothes and accessories.

Now, this place really felt like home.

"Do you want breakfast?" he asked.

"Depends."

He moved into the doorway of our bedroom. A pair of sweats sat low on his waist, showing the V that cut up the sides of his lower stomach, the abs that rode up the middle, and the dark hair that covered the top of his chest.

He was all man, and I loved every bit of it.

"Depends if we're going to the gym or not."

"And if we don't?"

"I want breakfast."

He laughed and disappeared into the kitchen. While I waited, I lifted my phone off the nightstand and pulled up one of my social media accounts. The first picture I came across was of Eve, and I double-tapped it. She had left Miami yesterday to go to New York City to style another one of her clients. The photo she'd posted was of her in a pizza shop, eating a slice that was larger than her arm.

I scrolled and saw a picture of Scarlett next. She was on a sailboat with Jack and some other people I didn't recognize. They were in Nassau for a few days, doing some business and taking a little time off for themselves.

I passed a few other shots of women I'd worked with in the past and girls I'd hung out with in LA. There were pictures of them at brunch and at the beach and having cocktails.

Things I didn't miss.

In a city I didn't miss at all.

It wasn't just Brett that kept me in Miami. I had absolutely no desire to return to LA. Not just because I didn't have any work there, but also because nothing had felt real. Or right. Or comfortable. Even the sunshine had felt more like a tanning bed than the heat that baked on us here.

I'd made the right choice.

I was reminded of that every morning when I woke up next to Brett—even if we still had to keep our relationship a secret.

Focusing on the screen again, I got past all the girl shots, and I came across a series of pictures that Max had posted sometime last night. The tag showed he was in Nashville, and I knew that meant he was at Sophia's concert. When I'd spoken to Eve yesterday morning, she'd told me that Max was going.

She wasn't happy about it, but there was nothing we could do. Sophia was part of The Agency, and that wasn't going to change.

I double-clicked the first shot, which was a selfie with Max standing backward on the stage, showing all the seats behind him at the Ryman. *Dream come true*, was the caption.

The next picture was of him and several other people, none I recognized, which were probably the members of Sophia's crew. The third shot was of him, Abel, and Sophia. I stared at it for several seconds, waiting to feel something.

I felt nothing.

No anger. No hatred. No sadness.

They didn't deserve any of that from me, and in the weeks that had passed since the party, everything I had felt for them completely left my body. Now, I saw Eve's boyfriend standing between two people I wanted nothing to do with.

I swiped once more and reached the last photo. This one was just of him and Sophia backstage with lots of crewmembers standing around in the background.

I knew Max wasn't trying to upset Eve by posting these pictures. He certainly wasn't trying to rub anything in my face. He wasn't like that. But Max was all business, just like Brett. He promoted his clients to gain them more interest, he wanted to be seen with them to make him a more desirable agent, and he wanted to plug the company every chance he got.

Social media was the perfect way to do it, and these guys were good at it.

It was just hard to believe that someone as bitchy as Sophia Sully could have such a large following. She hadn't reached full stardom yet, but she was well on her way, and Max was going to do everything he could to get her there.

She looked the part well with the curled blonde hair and the short cutoffs and the large, perfectly white teeth. She had everyone fooled, everyone believing she was an angel. I wished they had seen that angel when she locked me in the restroom at the party.

I couldn't think about it anymore.

My eyes shifted to the top of the photo, gazing at the faces of the people who were behind Sophia and Max. There were several in the left corner and in the middle and one on the right. Once my eyes landed on the right, they didn't move. Something about that guy looked familiar. I could only see three quarters of his face, but his jaw was one I remembered along with those short sideburns and that messy brown hair.

He was smiling, and I saw his teeth.

Large front teeth.

I shot up straight in bed, the blanket dropping to my waist, and I gasped in a breath and screamed, "Brett!"

Oh my God.

I couldn't believe what the hell I was looking at.

I couldn't believe, after all this time, I was finally seeing *his* face.

"Brett!" I yelled again.

"Yeah?"

"Get in here! Come quick!"

I heard his feet on the floor, and they got louder, the closer he got until he was in the doorway, saying, "What's wrong?"

I held out my phone, so he could see the screen. "That's him."

"Who?"

"That's fucking Calvin." I pointed at the photo, tapping the screen so hard that I was sure my nail broke. "Right there in Max's picture. I can't see that much of his face, but I don't need to. Brett, I'm positive it's him."

He grabbed the phone out of my hand. "Which one?"

"The guy on the right."

His jaw clenched, and his lip curled. Finally, he glanced up from my phone. "Why is Calvin backstage at Sophia's concert?"

I shook my head. "I don't know."

"Where the fuck is my phone?" He scanned the room until he located it on the dresser and lifted it into his hands. He hit the screen and tapped it a few times before holding it up to his ear. "I'm about to fuck somebody up."

34

BRETT

MAX DIDN'T ANSWER his phone until the third ring, and with a rough, scratchy voice, he said, "Brett, do you have any idea what fucking time it is? I went to bed two hours ago. Give me a goddamn break."

"Pull up those pictures you posted on social media last night." Using James's phone, I flipped through the stack he'd uploaded, so I could give him some direction. "And go to the last one."

"I'm going back to bed."

"Like hell you are."

"What's the point of this?"

"Just do it," I growled.

"I'm hungover as fuck. Give me a fucking second." I heard a click and his breathing. "What picture again? The one with—"

"You and Sophia."

He sighed. "Don't even tell me this phone call is about you being pissed that I went to her concert last night. Because, man, I've about reached my limit with all this Sophia bullshit."

I ground my teeth together, trying to calm my nerves before I exploded. "Max, just look at the fucking picture, and tell me who the guy is in the upper-right corner."

"The upper-right corner," he repeated. "Fuck, I've got to put in my contacts; I can't see shit. Hang on."

If Max were in Miami right now, I would get in my goddamn car and drive to his house and skip all of this. But Sophia was playing a two-night show in Nashville, so Max wasn't due back until tomorrow.

"Brett, what's he saying?" James asked. Since she'd shown me the picture on her phone, she'd covered her naked body with a pair of yoga pants and a tank top, and she was sitting in the middle of the bed, fidgeting nonstop.

"He's putting in his contacts; he can't fucking see."

She ran her hands through both sides of her hair. "Tell me you're kidding."

I shook my head, my jaw clenched so tightly that my head was pounding.

"All right, I'm back," he said.

"Who's the guy, Max?"

Several seconds passed before he said, "I don't know. I've never seen him before."

"Find out, and call me back. And do me a fucking favor; hurry the fuck up, or I'll be on the next flight to Nashville, and I'll find out myself."

"Brett, what the hell is going on?"

There was so much emotion on James's face, it was stabbing me in the chest.

"That guy in the photo is Calvin Parker."

The emotion doubled as soon as I said his name, and James tucked her knees against her chest and began to rock.

"Wait, you mean—"

"I mean, the same Calvin Parker who taped James and leaked their video to the entire world. Yeah, that motherfucker."

"Shit, Brett."

"Call me back," I barked. "Quickly."

"Give me an hour," he said, and he hung up.

I dropped the phone on the bed and crawled over the mattress until James was in my arms. I held her against my chest and placed my mouth on the top of her head in one long, endless kiss. "He's on it. We'll have an answer soon. I promise."

She was shaking. Her breathing was labored, and her tears were just starting to fall. No matter how hard she quivered, how much she cried, I didn't let her go until my phone beeped with a message. From where I sat, I could see there was a picture on the screen.

I grabbed my cell, clicked the photo to enlarge it, and held it out in front of us.

"Oh my God," she gasped. Her hand went over her mouth, her eyes moving from me to the photo and back.

It wasn't the same picture Max had uploaded to social media last night. This shot was a close-up of the guy's face. In many ways, it resembled the one the sketch artist had drawn at the police station, but I could tell where James's memory had been fuzzy, and in her description, not all of his characteristics had come through.

"Brett..." Her eyes were glued to the screen, and the emotion that poured through them fucking choked me. "That's him. That's fucking him." She placed her other hand on her chest and looked at me. "Who is he?"

"I have to call Max."

I got up from the bed, needing to feel the floor under my feet, and I pressed the button for his cell.

This time, he answered halfway through the first ring. "Is that him?"

"Yes," I growled.

"Jesus fucking Christ."

"Who is he? Fucking tell me."

"His name isn't Calvin Parker, but that should come as no surprise. His real name is Scott Watson. He lives in Gulfport, Mississippi, and runs security for a large casino in Biloxi. Turns out, Scott isn't just good with surveillance feed; he also dabbles in hacking."

"What aren't you telling me?"

I looked at James while I waited for his answer.

"Man, you were right," he said.

Anger began to boil in my chest. "Who the fuck is he, Max?"

"He's Sophia's half brother."

"Motherfucker..." I walked toward the bathroom, so James wouldn't see my face, and I tried to calm myself down before my fist went through the nearest piece of drywall. "We'll talk about this when I get home after our trip to LA. Right now, I want you to call our legal team and get the paperwork drawn up to terminate her contract. When the media finds out—and that's going to be soon—I don't want her name attached to The Agency."

"Brett—"

"Max, she broke the fucking law. Not to mention, she tried to destroy my client, who also happens to be my girlfriend. Had you not taken that picture, I don't know if we ever would have found out whom he was. So, don't fucking start with me about you not wanting to be like the other agents in LA. That cunt is finished, and once the media hears this, they're going to tear her to fucking shreds."

"I was just going to ask if you wanted me to meet you in LA to present the evidence I found."

With my back toward her, I leaned into the doorway of the bathroom. "Thanks, man. I'll let you know once I get there if I need you to fly out. Right now, if you could text the pilots and tell them I need them on the tarmac in an hour, that would be a lot of help."

"You got it."

I disconnected the call and shoved my phone into the pocket of my sweats, my other hand raking through my morning hair. I didn't want to turn around; I didn't want to see the look on her face. But I fucking had to.

She was sitting at the end of the mattress, looking pale as hell.

"James..."

She wrapped her arms around her stomach, and her lips parted for several seconds before she said, "Sophia set this up, didn't she?"

I nodded. "He's her half brother."

"Oh my God. I think I'm going to be sick."

I moved over to the bed and knelt in front of her, resting my hands on her thighs. "Listen to me, before I call the detective, I want you to know everything Max told me, but I need to know you're ready to hear it. The last thing I want right now is to make you hurt more. So, if you need a second, I understand."

She put her hand on mine. The gesture wasn't for affection; it felt more like she needed to hold on to something. "I want to hear it."

"You're sure?"

"Yes."

I waited a few seconds in case she changed her mind. When she said nothing, I started with, "The guy's name is Scott Watson. He works in security for a casino in Mississippi, so he understands surveillance and camera systems. It's how he was able to manipulate the feed at the Malibu hotel."

She was getting paler, and I had no idea how to make her feel better because the news was only about to get worse.

"According to someone Max spoke to, Scott also does hacking on the side. I know that's how he was able to leak the video without it being traced. I'm sure he uploaded it to the dark net on an offshore server, and someone was more than happy to send it to where it needed to go. He'd just edited his face and voice first."

"She wanted to ruin me." Her voice was just a little above a whisper. "She knew I'd be vulnerable at that party, and she had Calvin—or Scott or whatever the hell his name is hit on me in hopes that I'd sleep with him. And..." She swallowed and took a breath, holding her chest like that was helping her fill her lungs. "And I fell for it. I did everything she wanted me to. What the fuck is wrong with me, Brett? How could I be so stupid?"

I squeezed her thighs and shook them. "Jesus, James, this isn't your fault. She manipulated you, and there was no way you could have known. And, if you hadn't fallen then, she would have tried again. She was determined to make your life hell, and she wouldn't have given up until she accomplished it."

"What did I do to her?"

I shook my head. "I don't know, baby. But she's not getting away with it. I'm going to call the detective, and then we're getting on a plane and flying to LA. We'll tell him everything we just found out, so he can do what he needs to in order to take them down."

"It's over." She looked up at the ceiling, tears streaming down her cheeks. "Brett, it's over."

I wrapped my arms around her waist and pulled her so fucking close, trying to take some of the pain away.

"It's over," she whispered again, as though she were having a hard time believing it.

"I can't wait for that cunt to get what's coming to her."

She released my shoulders and leaned back to look at my face. "Make the call."

I got up from the floor and took my phone out of my pocket. I searched for the number I'd saved after James and I left the police station. "Detective, it's Brett Young," I said once he answered.

"Mr. Young." I could tell I had woken him up. With the time

difference, it was only a little past four in the morning in LA. "I'm hoping this call means you have some information."

"The man in the video isn't Calvin Parker. His real name is Scott Watson, and he's Sophia Sully's half brother."

"You're positive?"

"James identified him this morning in a picture on social media. He was in a shot with one of my agents at Sophia's concert in Nashville. I had my agent look into it, and he got some information on Scott."

"How quickly can you get here?"

"We'll be boarding in less than an hour."

"Text me when you land. I'll meet you at the police station."

I dropped my phone on the dresser and went back to the bed to lift her into my arms. She didn't fight me at all; she just fell against my chest and clung her arms around me.

"We're getting in the shower, and then we're going to the airport."

35

BRETT

AS I WAS GRABBING some coffee in the kitchen, I heard a soft knock come from the front of my penthouse. Leaving the mug on the counter, I went into the foyer and opened the door.

"Mr. Young, here are the newspapers you requested," the doorman said.

I took the stack he handed to me and thanked him before he rode my private elevator down to the lobby.

Lifting my coffee back in my hand, I scanned the headlines and made my way to the bedroom. Once I got inside, I flipped on the light and crawled into bed.

"Just a few more minutes," James grumbled, turning away from the lamp and tucking the blanket over her head.

The flying back and forth to LA, all the hours we'd spent at the police station, and the long dinner we'd had with Tim had really tired her out.

"Baby, you're going to want to wake up and see this."

Slowly, she pulled the comforter back, and her eyes opened. As she saw the papers in my lap, she sat up and turned toward me. "It's hit the news already?"

"Every major outlet." I dropped a newspaper in her hands. *"Los Angeles Times."* And then another. *"USA Today."* I gave her the last of the stack. *"New York Times. Washington Post. Miami Herald.* And every article is on the front page."

"Oh my God."

It wasn't even seven in the morning, but if I turned on the TV, I was sure every news channel would be reporting the story. The same would be true if I opened the internet. I glanced at my phone as it rested on my nightstand, and I saw alerts filling the screen, mentioning Sophia and James.

The truth had gone viral.

"Brett," she gasped as she read one of the articles. "You're not going to believe this."

With her facing me, I wasn't able to see the paper, so I said, "Read it to me."

"One of our reporters was on location in Biloxi, Mississippi, when Scott Watson was arrested. As he was being taken into police custody, we asked him what his motive was for taping and leaking the video. He responded, 'My sister paid me to do it. I can show you the bank deposit to prove it. She gave me one hundred thousand dollars to have sex with the hottest actress in the world. Of course I took the money. Who wouldn't?'" James looked at me. "My hate toward Sophia just reached a whole new level."

I knew that last part came from her, not the article.

"Keep reading," I said.

"'My sister asked me to humiliate James. You know, like spank her and give it to her rough—things that would cause her a little pain. That was my original plan. But, once I got her to the hotel room, I knew I couldn't go through with it. James is a real sweet girl, who just found herself in an unfortunate situation.'" She glanced up again. "An unfortunate situation? That's what it's called? I want to kill her...and him."

I rubbed my hands over her legs to try to calm her down.

"Remember, every word that comes out of that moron's mouth only helps your case. But he's a fucking idiot. I bet he thinks, by throwing Sophia under the bus, it'll take some of the heat off of him. Damn, he is so wrong."

"She's legitimately crazy."

I laughed because, out of all the women I'd met in this industry, some whose sanity I'd questioned, Sophia certainly trumped them all. "The world knows that now. I guarantee, if you open your social media, they're tearing her apart, but they're saying some pretty nice shit about you."

"She must really love Abel to go through all that."

"That's not love, James. That's obsession. The chick needs some help, and maybe now, she'll get it." I looked at the newspaper she had sitting in her lap and held my hand out. "I want to see what else they're saying."

She gave it to me, and I started reading.

THE MALE PARTNER IN THE INTERNATIONALLY DISTRIBUTED SEX TAPE OF ACTRESS JAMES RYNE HAS BEEN IDENTIFIED AS SCOTT WATSON OF GULFPORT, MISSISSIPPI. WATSON HAS BEEN ARRESTED ON SEVERAL COUNTS, INCLUDING RECORDING A SEXUAL ACT WITHOUT CONSENT, DISTRIBUTION OF THE SEXUAL ACT WITHOUT PERMISSION, EXPLOITATION, AND INVASION OF PRIVACY.

WATSON, 26, IS THE HALF BROTHER OF COUNTRY SINGER SOPHIA SULLY. SULLY, 22, IS CURRENTLY ENGAGED TO ABEL CURRY, 18, AND ACCORDING TO THE INFORMATION THAT HAS BEEN RELEASED, WE UNDERSTAND THEIR RELATIONSHIP BEGAN WHILE HE WAS STILL DATING RYNE.

SULLY IS CURRENTLY ON TOUR FOR HER LATEST ALBUM, BLUE-TOED BOOTS, AND HAS YET TO RESPOND TO HER HALF BROTHER'S ALLEGATIONS THAT SHE PAID HIM TO HAVE SEXUAL RELATIONS WITH RYNE, TO FILM THOSE RELATIONS,

AND TO DISTRIBUTE THE VIDEO WORLDWIDE. SULLY'S
MOTIVES ARE STILL UNCLEAR.
WHEN WE REACHED OUT TO HER TEAM, THEY INFORMED US
THEY NO LONGER REPRESENT THE SINGER. WE HAVE
REACHED OUT TO SULLY PERSONALLY AND HAVE YET TO
RECEIVE A RESPONSE.

I set the paper down and wrapped my arms around her neck, pressing my lips against her forehead. "I like the part that says she no longer has a team. Karma is such a cunt."

"I wish I could have seen her face when all of this went down."

My phone beeped from the nightstand, and I saw a celebrity alert on the screen. "Hang on, I might be able to show it to you." I grabbed the phone and held it in front of us.

BREAKING NEWS:

SOPHIA SULLY HAS BEEN TAKEN INTO CUSTODY TO BE
QUESTIONED IN THE JAMES RYNE SEX TAPE SCANDAL.
WONDER HOW SHE'S GOING TO SING HERSELF OUT OF
THIS ONE.

Underneath the alert was a picture of Sophia. She had on large sunglasses and was using her hand to try to block her face from the cameras. The scowl she had on was fucking priceless.

James's eyes met mine, and she said, "I feel like my entire life has just changed. Again."

My phone went off a second time with another celebrity alert. This one also had a picture, but it was a shot of James from the first gala she'd attended as a client of The Agency when she wore that subtly sexy, long black dress.

AMERICA'S SWEETHEART, IT'S TIME TO DUST OFF YOUR

CROWN. WE HAVE A FEELING YOU'LL BE PUTTING IT ON
AGAIN REAL SOON.
AND, GIRL, WE'D SAY YOU EARNED IT.

"Baby," I said, waiting for her stare to return to me. I moved my lips so goddamn close to hers, and I whispered, "You're right; it has changed again. But, now, you have me, and it's only going to get so much better."

36

JAMES

Abel: I know you're probably shocked to hear from me, but I'm reaching out because I owe you an apology.
Me: It's a little too late for an apology, don't you think?
Abel: It is, but, God, James, she was always so jealous of you. I should have known how deep her jealousy ran when she wouldn't let me be at the house on the day you moved out. I told you I had to film, but that was a lie. She used to check my phone every day to see if you'd called or texted. I tried to delete whatever had come in, but sometimes, I didn't have a chance. Those messages would set her off for days, and I'd have to listen to her bitch about you nonstop. For what it's worth, I didn't know Sophia and Scott were involved in the video. But then you came up to us at that party in Miami, and the guy you were describing sounded like Scott. I never saw the two of you together, but I knew he was there that night. I should have told you when you asked. I'm sorry I didn't.
Me: You're right. You should have told me.
Abel: I know I've fucked up a lot, and I'm not proud of those mistakes.

Me: We've both made mistakes we're not proud of, Abel. I just want to know where we went wrong.

Abel: We were so young when we got together, and you were the only girl I'd ever been with. We both got so busy, and you were traveling a lot for press tours and filming. Our lives were moving in opposite directions. Sophia just happened to be there.

Me: Wow.

Abel: I just wanted you to know how fucking sorry I am that all of this happened.

Me: Apology accepted. Take care.

37

JAMES

I WAS SITTING on a high-top stool in the green room of *The Ellen DeGeneres Show* while a makeup artist touched up my eye shadow and a hairstylist re-curled all my strands.

Tim had stopped by when I first arrived to bring me a bouquet of flowers. I hadn't seen him since the announcement of the movie deal, and he had come to congratulate me. Eve had also popped in to help me get dressed, making sure the accessories she had chosen coordinated as well as she wanted them to.

They did.

The gold jewelry went perfectly with my navy dress, and the sparkly stilettos were just so fun. Unfortunately, Eve wasn't able to stay for the show. She had to catch a flight to New York, but I'd be seeing her in Miami in a few weeks.

"Two-minute countdown," an assistant said after opening the door and peeking his head in.

"I'll be ready," I told him.

"Can I have a second alone with her, ladies?" Brett said as he got up from the couch and walked over to me. He didn't touch me until both girls were gone. "This dress," he growled, running his hands over my sides and across my stomach before finally landing on my neck, "is going to be on the floor of the plane the second I get you on board."

I smiled, turning my face so that he wouldn't kiss me on the lips. "Brett, no," I said, laughing as he tried to move my chin. "You can't smudge my gloss when I'm about to go onstage."

"Look at me," he demanded.

Slowly, I turned my mouth toward him, anticipating his to immediately press against mine.

But it didn't.

It just hovered close as he said, "I want you to go out there and fucking kill it."

"I remember you saying something like that once before."

"Mmm," he moaned, grazing his lips across my collarbone. Once they left my skin, I felt the goose bumps rise. "And look what happened; you went into that meeting, and you fucking killed it."

I smiled. "I did okay."

"I love how humble you are."

And I love you.

Neither of us had said that yet.

But I felt his love, and I knew he felt mine.

"I have to go," I said, wiggling forward to back him up.

He held my hand while I climbed off the stool, and he walked me to the door. "I'm going to watch backstage."

"Good." I air-kissed my finger and pressed it against his lips. "I'll see you in a little bit."

The assistant who had come in to tell me how much time was left was waiting in the hall, not far from my door. I joined him, and he brought me through the production area and told me to wait on the side of the stage.

"There's going to be a twenty-second countdown that will show right there." He pointed at a digital screen on the wall next to me. "When there are seven seconds to go, you'll hear the music start to play, and Ellen will announce you. When she does, it's your time to enter the set. Don't walk out before she says your name. I'll be here to give you the signal just in case you forget."

"Thank you."

Appearing on talk shows always made me nervous because, even though a list of questions had been sent to my publicist, the host often went off script and asked whatever came to their mind. Given the last several months of my life, I suspected that would happen today.

The clock on the wall lit up with a twenty-second countdown.

I clenched my hands and released them, feeling how sweaty my palms were. I tried taking deep breaths to calm the nerves in my stomach. I wiggled my toes, so the heels loosened and felt more comfortable.

Twelve seconds.

I reminded myself that I'd done multiple interviews over the last two months, and those had been much harder than this one would be. So, today was about celebrating. It was about being grateful for this opportunity. It was about remembering how kind and generous the public had become.

The music started to play, and the assistant looked at me, using his fingers to show the countdown of seconds.

I heard clapping on set.

I heard tons of cheering.

Four seconds.

The assistant urged me to take a few steps forward to get closer to the stage.

Two seconds.

The noise on set got louder.

One second.

"For today's show, I'm so honored to welcome the beautiful and talented James Ryne," Ellen said.

Go, the assistant mouthed.

I felt my feet on the ground, and my arms move through the air as I held my breath. The lights got brighter as I stepped on the hardwood floor of the stage, and the sounds got much more intense. I rounded the corner that was hidden behind a partition and saw the crowd.

They were standing. They were clapping. They were all smiling at me.

I was hit with their energy.

Their enthusiasm.

Their love.

I smiled back at all of them. I waved with both hands, and I shimmied my hips and shoulders to the music as I walked toward the sitting area on set. Once I got a little closer to Ellen, I turned my stare toward her. Her smile was just as big as the crowd, and it calmed me a little.

Even though we had never met in person, I bypassed the handshake and went right in for a hug. "Thank you so much for having me," I whispered.

"It's so great to meet you," she replied.

We pulled away from each other, and I moved in front of my seat, looking at the crowd again, still feeling all of their emotions. The grin on my face was ridiculously big.

"Thank you," I said to all of them.

And they clapped harder.

Ellen asked me to take a seat, and she waited for the audience to quiet down before she said, "Thanks for being here, James. We're really happy you were able to fit us in. I know things have been extremely busy for you."

I crossed my ankles, making sure my dress was resting flat, and folded my hands on my lap. "It might have been just a little hectic during a short period of time"—I smiled again, so they knew I was joking—"but I'm so excited to be here." I glanced at the crowd. "Thank you for giving me such a warm welcome."

There was another round of applause.

"This morning, while I was getting ready in my dressing room, I heard something pretty wonderful that I don't think the public knows yet." Suddenly, the screen behind our chairs showed a picture of Ralph and me. "Look who's been casted as the lead actress in the next Ralph Anderson film."

I took in the audience's clapping and felt my face turn a little red. "It's great news, isn't it? I'm such a huge fan of his, and to get a role in one of his movies is a dream come true."

"As my followers know, I make it no secret that I'm his biggest fan, too." The picture changed; it showed my face had been cropped out, and Ellen's was put there instead.

"You look great as a brunette," I said.

"Even with the longer hair?"

"Come on, guys," I directed at the crowd, "don't you think she looks fabulous with long, dark hair?"

More cheering erupted.

Once it became quiet again, Ellen said, "I've heard Ralph takes a nontraditional approach when he holds auditions."

"He does," I said and faced the audience, remembering both times I'd met with him and how different they were.

The first was when I'd reenacted the scene from *Burnt Away*, when my personal life was still a mess. The second time was when I'd landed my current role.

"Usually, your agent sets up an audition, and in a roomful of people and a few cameras, you read a short script." I gazed back at Ellen. "That's not how Ralph does it. He holds the audition in his office, and it's just him, you, and your agent in a room with no cameras." I used the armrests to push myself up. "We weren't able to meet at Ralph's office for my second audition, so my agent and I went to his house. We were outside on his patio, waiting for him, and it was such a hot day in LA. I was sweating. I mean, I was dripping buckets. I was nervous. I was guzzling water, and then I realized I'd not only emptied my glass, but I'd also finished my agent's glass, too."

"Your poor bladder."

"That's exactly the problem, Ellen. The second Ralph came outside, I had to pee. It was the kind of emergency where I had to cross my legs and sway my body. You girls know what I'm talking about, right?" I laughed from how hard Ellen was laughing. "So, Ralph and I talked about the scene he wanted me to act, and it required lots of walking and sitting. The whole time I was acting, I was trying so hard not to concentrate on how badly I had to go to the bathroom. But, now, I was sweating more; it was starting to show through my shirt, and my feet were slipping in my shoes." I giggled as the audience's laugher got louder.

"Did the scene call for any crying?"

"It did." I turned toward the crowd. "But my bladder was so full, I wanted to cry anyway. I guess you could say it worked out perfectly."

"Should we call Ralph and tell him what happened?"

"I caved and had to tell him when the scene was over. I couldn't have held it a second longer, or I don't know that I would have made it to the bathroom. Can you imagine? No, let's not imagine. Let's just be glad I made it in time."

"Did you happen to snap a photo of the bathroom? I want to make sure the ones in my house are up to par."

"I didn't, but he had some wonderful hand soap."

"Flowery?"

I smiled. "No, this was more like the scent of the beach."

"It sounds like his soap is nicer than mine."

"And mine," I assured her.

She waited for the laughter to die down and then said, "I've been following the news surrounding Sophia Sully and her half brother, Scott Watson. Is there any new information you can give us?"

This was the question I had known was coming but was afraid of.

The trial hadn't started, and it wouldn't for several months, but the evidence had been pouring in. The police had searched Scott's computer and found the video, where it had been uploaded, and how it had been distributed. The check Sophia had written to him for a hundred thousand dollars had been located, and now, she was being charged as an accessory.

My attorneys didn't know what their punishments would be, but they were sure Scott would at least receive some jail time.

As for Sophia, the damage to her career had already been done. She'd been dropped by The Agency, her label, and the rest of her team. Abel had broken off their engagement. Her remaining tour dates had been canceled, and her record sales had tanked.

The last photo that had been taken of her was a shot of her moving out of Abel's house.

I knew how that felt.

And I had no sympathy for her whatsoever.

"I have an incredible team of attorneys who are working hard on this case, and they're determined to get justice. It's all in their hands at this point." I took a deep breath. "But I will say this; I realize my actions that night weren't necessarily appropriate, but it doesn't matter who you are; we all deserve the right to privacy."

Ellen nodded in agreement and said, "After the verdict, will you come back on the show and celebrate with us?"

It felt good to hear she was on my side.

"I would love to," I said.

"Speaking of love, we haven't seen you date anyone since

Abel Curry. The audience is dying to know if there's someone special in your life."

It turned loud again for several seconds and then quieted.

Two months had passed since Scott was arrested, and my career was better now than ever before. I hadn't just landed a role in one of Ralph's movies, but Brett had also scored me another lead in a movie that one of his friends was directing. Endorsement deals were rolling in, I was looking into businesses that were seeking investors, and I'd just started my first online class.

Enough time had passed since the truth came out.

So had my nineteenth birthday.

I didn't want to keep it a secret anymore.

I felt my face blush again, a smile forming over my lips. "I do have someone in my life."

As the crowd roared, I glanced to the other side of the stage, which was open so that the production staff could see the set. Brett was standing all the way to the right with his hands in the pockets of his sexy navy suit. His smile lines dented his shortly trimmed beard. His teeth chewed the corner of his lip, and he was shaking his head at me.

I hadn't told him I was going to out us.

But I was sure he knew.

And nothing on his face told me he was disappointed.

"He came here with me today," I said, looking at the audience and then at Ellen. "And he's pretty amazing."

EPILOGUE

BRETT

JAMES and I sat next to each other in the third row from the stage in the Dolby Theatre in Hollywood. Tonight was the Oscars, and she had been nominated for her work in Ralph Anderson's film. I had known she was going to catch the attention of the Academy. Her performance in *Black Season* was outstanding, better than any of us could have anticipated. And Ralph was so pleased, he wanted to cast her again.

She didn't know that yet.

I wanted her to get through tonight before I gave her that news.

Knowing we were getting close to the presentation of the award, I reached across her lap and held her hand. She squeezed my fingers, and I saw two TV cameras move in front of where we were sitting. That was so they could get a shot of James's face when her name was announced as a nominee.

The host introduced a guest presenter, and an actor walked onstage, who had been James's costar in the film.

He held an envelope in his hand and waited for the audience to quiet before he read from the teleprompter. "The nominees for

Best Actress in a Motion Picture—Drama are James Ryne, *Black Season*."

The screen behind the podium showed a scene from the movie where James was in bed. She had no makeup on, her hair was wild, the blanket was falling from her body, and the clothes she had on underneath were tattered.

"She can't do this to me!" James screamed. "She can't hurt me anymore. I won't let her. I won't let her take my family." Tears streamed from her eyes. Spit soaked her lips.

The shot zoomed out, and the audience applauded right before her costar announced the next nominee.

I saw the red light flashing from the camera, signaling it was on and filming, and I knew there was a chance my face would be shown on TV. I didn't have a problem with it. Our relationship had been public for almost a year. James and I had walked many red carpets together, like the one we'd been on tonight, and we'd been photographed all over the world.

I wanted everyone to know that the gorgeous girl sitting to my left was mine. And I was so fucking proud of her.

"And the Oscar goes to..."

I squeezed her hand again.

"James Ryne, *Black Season*."

"Brett..." she whispered.

She turned toward me, her mouth open, shock filling her beautiful face. I continued to hold her hand, and I got up to help her stand. Right before she walked away, she leaned in and kissed me. Then, she made her way up the stairs and hugged her costar before she went over to the podium.

"Wow, I didn't expect this, and because of that, I didn't write anything down." I heard the emotion in her voice, and then she paused. "To my fellow nominees, women who are so incredibly talented, thank you for being such an inspiration to my career." Her chest rose as she took a breath. "Ralph Anderson, thank you for taking a chance on me. For giving me the role of my dreams, for mentoring me, and for helping me become the actress I am today." She glanced up toward the ceiling. "For my parents, whom I lost far too soon, I hope you're looking down on me and I'm making you proud." She gazed into the audience again. "To the team of actors and actresses and the production staff and everyone who was involved in the making of this movie, I certainly couldn't have done this without you." She searched the rows of seats until our eyes met. "To my team—Tim, Eve, all the wonderful people at The Agency, and to my agent, Brett Young."

She smiled at me, and my fucking heart beat so goddamn hard.

"Brett, I love you so much. The best thing I ever did was sign with you."

She thanked the crowd and the Academy and grinned one last time.

As she was escorted offstage, I watched her ass. It looked so fucking sexy in that dress. I had a feeling I'd be fucking it in between after-parties tonight. There was no way in hell I could wait until we got back to The Agency's condo.

The music began to play throughout the room, which told all the attendees the network was taking a commercial break, and my phone immediately started blowing up. I grabbed it from the inside pocket of my tux and checked the screen.

Scarlett: Just saw you on TV. I know you don't want to hear this, but the whole world melted when they saw you smile at her onstage. Give that girl a big hug for me.

Max: Turn around, and look toward your left.

I did as Max had asked, scanning the rows behind me until I

saw him and Eve toward the back. I waved at them and checked my phone again as it vibrated.

Max: We'll meet you at the after-party. We're so fucking proud of her.

Jack: I told you a while ago that you'd be a fool not to take her on. I'm glad you listened. I'm proud of her. I'm even prouder of you, motherfucker. See you later tonight.

I leaned to the side of my chair and took out my wallet, reaching into the front section where I kept the small piece of paper.

YOU'D BE A FOOL NOT TO TAKE HER ON.

Those were the words written on it, and they had come from Jack. He'd given me that note when James came into our conference room for the very first time and told us what had happened in Malibu. Back then, I'd stared at the sheet for several seconds, wondering if he was right. And then, slowly, I'd made eye contact with James. That was when I'd kicked everyone out and had my one-on-one with her.

James knew about the piece of paper because, on the night I'd proposed to her, I'd slipped it through the ring, and both had sat in the middle of my hand as I got down on one knee.

The ring was now on her finger, but the paper would always stay with me.

Have you read ...
Endorsed—*Jack's book*
Contracted—*Max's book*
Negotiated—*Scarlett's Novella*

ACKNOWLEDGMENTS

Jovana Shirley, you're the best. I truly can't say that enough. I've never met anyone who understands my stories like you do and who treats my words with so much love. You're stuck with me forever. XO.

Nina Grinstead, thanks for believing in me, for talking me off every ledge, for being the best partner in crime. I wouldn't want to do this with anyone but you.

Judy Zweifel, you are such a treasure, and I appreciate you so much. Thanks for all the love.

Letitia Hasser, thank you for always understanding my vision and for giving my babies the most stunning faces.

Ricky, my sexyreads, my soul sister, I can't live without you. I love you, I love you, I love you. #MyFistingBestie #TheWhiteStuff

Kaitie Reister, thank you for being my second set of eyes. Love you so much, girlie.

Kimmi Street, you held my hand throughout this whole book, and, babe, I needed it. You always have my back, and you always know what's best for my heart. I'm so lucky to have a bestie like you. Love you so much.

Crystal Radaker, I don't know what I would do without you. You keep me sane and inspired, and our chats are seriously epic. Thanks for being on this journey with me. Love you tons.

Donna Cooksley Sanderson, thanks for all of your support. Love you, lady. XX.

Extra-special love goes to Stacey Jacovina, Jesse James, Kayti McGee, Carol Nevarez, Julie Vaden, Elizabeth Kelley, RC Boldt, Jennifer Porpora, Melissa Mann, Katie Amanatidis, my COPA ladies, and my group of Sarasota girls whom I love more than anything. I'm so grateful for all of you.

Mom and Dad, thanks for your unwavering belief in me and your constant encouragement. It means more than you'll ever know.

Brian, my words could never dent the amount of love you give me. Trust me when I say, I love you more.

My Midnighters, you are such a supportive, loving, motivating group. Thanks for being such an inspiration, for holding my hand when I need it, and for always begging for more words. I love you all.

To all the bloggers who read, review, share, post, tweet, Instagram—Thank you, thank you, thank you will never be enough. You do so much for our writing community, and we're so appreciative.

To my readers—I cherish each and every one of you. I'm so grateful for all the love you show my books, for taking the time to reach out to me, and for your passion and enthusiasm. I love, love, love you.

BONUS SCENE

Do you want more of James and Brett from *Signed*? If so, please sign up for my newsletter, and I'll send you an exclusive bonus scene that isn't available anywhere else.

CLICK HERE

MARNI'S MIDNIGHTERS

Getting to know my readers is one of my favorite parts about being an author. In Marni's Midnighters, my private Facebook group, we chat about steamy books, sexy and taboo toys, and sensual book boyfriends. Team members also qualify for exclusive giveaways and are the first to receive sneak peeks of the projects I'm currently working on. To join Marni's Midnighters, click HERE.

ABOUT THE AUTHOR

USA Today best-selling author Marni Mann knew she was going to be a writer since middle school. While other girls her age were daydreaming about teenage pop stars, Marni was fantasizing about penning her first novel. She crafts sexy, titillating stories that weave together her love of darkness, mystery, passion, and human emotions. A New Englander at heart, she now lives in Sarasota, Florida, with her husband and their two dogs. When she's not nose deep in her laptop, working on her next novel, she's scouring for chocolate, sipping wine, traveling, or devouring fabulous books.

Want to get in touch? Visit Marni at ...
www.marnismann.com
MarniMannBooks@gmail.com

ALSO BY MARNI MANN

THE AGENCY STAND-ALONE SERIES—Erotic Romance

Signed

Endorsed

Contracted

Negotiated

STAND-ALONE NOVELS

The Assistant (Contemporary Romance)

When Ashes Fall (Contemporary Romance)

The Unblocked Collection (Erotic Romance)

Wild Aces (Erotic Romance)

Prisoned (Dark Erotic Thriller)

THE SHADOWS SERIES—Erotic Romance

Seductive Shadows—Book One

Seductive Secrecy—Book Two

THE PRISONED SPIN-OFF DUET—Dark Erotic Thriller

Animal—Book One

Monster—Book Two

THE BAR HARBOR SERIES—New Adult

Pulled Beneath—Book One

Pulled Within—Book Two

THE MEMOIR SERIES—Dark Mainstream Fiction

Memoirs Aren't Fairytales—Book One

Scars from a Memoir—Book Two

NOVELS COWRITTEN WITH GIA RILEY

Lover (Erotic Romance)

Drowning (Contemporary Romance)

SNEAK PEEK OF ENDORSED

JACK - SEVEN YEARS AGO

"FOR THE FIFTH overall pick in this year's NFL draft, the Tennessee Titans choose Shawn Cole, tight end from Florida State," the NFL commissioner announced as he stood on the stage.

Once my client's name was called, I got up from my chair and cheered as loud as Shawn's family. "That's our boy," I said, gripping the shoulders of Shawn's dad and shaking them.

All that fucking work had paid off.

It wasn't just the hours I'd logged from trying to convince Shawn that I was the best agent for him, something I'd pushed since the last day of his college football season, but it was also the months of negotiation it had taken to get him an NFL contract.

It was all worth it.

Shawn, smiling like the richest motherfucker, stood and hugged his mother first. He then moved to his three older sisters. The fourth and youngest sister, Samantha—a girl I'd been secretly fooling around with since I met her three days ago—he hugged next. And then, finally, he embraced his dad.

I was sitting the farthest away, and he reached me last.

He shook my hand and patted my arm as he hugged me. "We did it, man."

"You did it." I pulled back. "Now, go show the world why you deserve to be a Titan."

Shawn followed my order, climbing the steps and walking onto the stage. A Titans hat was immediately placed on his head, and a jersey with his name and number was handed to him. He held the jersey in front of him, his smile growing even larger as he turned it, so the audience could see both sides.

The cheering erupted.

I took a quick peek at Samantha. She had her hand over her mouth; those gorgeous, dark eyes were wide and emotional as she stared at her brother.

I'd told his family that Shawn would get drafted in the top twenty.

But fifth?

I couldn't fucking believe it.

Besides a few small endorsement deals and a soccer contract, this was my first big break. One that would get my name printed on every sports page across America. One that would prove to my boss that, even though I'd just recently graduated from college, I would continue working my ass off until I was the top sports agent in LA.

As I glanced back at Shawn, where he was now posing in front of the camera, my phone vibrated from inside my suit. I pulled it out, the screen lighting up with texts from Max and Brett and Scarlett—my best friends, who all worked at the same agency as me. Their messages congratulated me on the Titans contract and said we'd celebrate tomorrow when I got back to California. Before putting my cell away, an email came through. It was from the Titans, and it outlined Shawn's schedule and what was required of him in the next few days.

I reviewed it all and slipped the phone into my pocket,

waiting for Shawn to reach our aisle before I said, "Are you ready to get back to work?"

"Hell yeah."

"The Titans want you to report to their training facility tomorrow afternoon. That means, instead of flying home to Florida, you'll be heading to Nashville."

"I'm down for whatever they want."

"Good," I said, pounding his fist. "Then, tonight, we celebrate."

"Tonight, we're getting fucking drunk," he promised.

And, hell, he kept that goddamn promise.

By one that morning, Samantha and I wanted to slip out of the bar and go back to our hotel for some alone time. We'd partied enough. So, she mentioned to her family that she was ready to go to bed, and I told Shawn I would escort her to the hotel.

I hadn't been able to keep my fucking hands off her, and after three days of foreplay, I was ready for more.

She was the most beautiful girl I'd ever seen. She didn't just deserve my attention; her presence demanded it.

And she had all of it—my hands and my mouth whenever one of her family members wasn't looking, my stare even if they were.

And, now, we were going to be by ourselves, and we wouldn't have to hide what we were doing.

I held her hand while we caught a taxi outside the bar in lower Manhattan, and we were driven to Midtown. We stumbled out of the back seat, and as I walked her into the lobby, my arm snaked around her waist.

"Shawn is going to be *sooo* far away now," she slurred.

I wasn't paying attention to her words. I was too focused on her body. As I held it tightly against my side, I was so turned on. Her heat, her smell, her touch—I wanted more, and I wanted it now.

"Nashville isn't even close to Florida, and I'm all the way down in Miami," she continued. "How will I see his games?"

"Your brother will be making enough that he can fly you there every weekend."

"You think?"

As we reached the elevator, I hit the button to take us upstairs. "I know."

"But he could get cut, couldn't he? And then what would happen?"

I turned her toward me. Those thick, glossy lips were begging me to kiss them. "Then, I'd find him a new team. But that's not going to happen. He's too good."

"You're so sure."

I put my hand on the back of her head, tilting her face up to mine. "Tennessee just lost one of their starting tight ends. They need someone with your brother's height and speed and with hands as quick as his. As long as he doesn't get injured during camp, he's got the starting spot."

"You're so sexy when you talk football."

I gripped her harder, my mouth moving closer to hers until I heard the elevator open. Then, my hand dropped to her waist again, and I led her inside, hitting the button for my floor. My room was where she'd chosen to hang out tonight.

"Make it move faster," she said, referring to the speed in which we were climbing.

She wrapped her hands around my arm, and she licked across her top lip. I couldn't pull my fucking eyes away.

It was so hard to make sure her brother had been occupied each time I kissed her. But at six-six, Shawn had three inches and a good thirty pounds on me. He was my top client. I sure as fuck didn't want him to see me all over his nineteen-year-old sister, who lived on the opposite side of the country as me, attending school at the University of Miami.

I didn't have to worry about that anymore.

"You think you have another drink in you?"

She hiccuped. "I know I do." I laughed, and she grabbed the lapels of my suit. "I majored in partying last semester. You know, all freshmen do their first year in college."

"I remember. I was one once."

The door slid open, and I brought her to my room. Once we were inside, she went to the minibar and scanned the shelves. She pulled out four small bottles of vodka and held them in the air.

"These will do," she said, handing me two and then climbing on top of the bed, gently bouncing while she guzzled the first one. Once the small bottle was empty, she dropped it onto the mattress and opened the second one. Right before it reached her mouth, she jumped, and the vodka splashed out. Some landed on her face and the rest on her shirt.

"Oh my God," she screeched, using her sleeve to wipe it off her skin.

I set both of my bottles on the dresser—one full, the other in my stomach. I'd taken it down like a shot as I watched her jump, her fucking nipples hardening more with each bounce.

"I'll get you a towel."

I went into the bathroom, grabbing the hand towel by the sink, and I returned to the bed.

Samantha was sitting on the mattress with her shirt off, holding it up in the air for me to see. "It's soaked."

The only thing I was focused on was her tits. They were held tightly in a black strapless bra, her pink nipples poking through the lace.

Jesus, fuck.

She had curves. She had the smoothest-looking skin. She had the kind of body I wanted to worship, that I wanted to taste until my tongue was too tired to lick anymore.

"Do you want a T-shirt to put on?"

She shook her head, and I took several steps closer until I stood in front of her. Using my knee, I slid her legs apart and moved in between them.

I wanted her bra off.

I wanted her jeans on my goddamn floor.

I wanted her lips around the end of my cock.

She was Shawn's sister, and I was playing with fucking fire.

"You have way too much on." Her hands went to my belt, and she unhooked it, unbuttoning and unzipping my suit pants. As they fell to the floor, she started on my jacket and shirt, and suddenly, I had on only a T-shirt and my boxer briefs.

I ran my fingers across her cheek, the look in her eyes telling me she was waiting for me to make the next move. My thumb then dipped lower and found a slick spot on her chin, a place she must have missed where the vodka had spilled. I brought my thumb up to my mouth and licked it off.

"Your brother can never know what happens in here. If he ever found out, it could ruin my career."

"I know." She blushed. "I'm going to go wash my face."

I stopped myself from putting my hand back on her. "Go do that."

She slid to the side and slowly rose from the bed.

"Fuck," I groaned as I watched her take a step, her smile pulling me in as much as her tits. "Your body is incredible."

She stood next to me, and I turned toward her. She ran her hands up her sides until they landed on her tits, two fingers brushing over her nipples.

The liquor had made her more confident.

I liked this version, and I liked how innocent she had acted before she started drinking.

But this sexual side was hot as hell, and it was fucking

dangerous. My cock didn't seem to care; the goddamn thing was so hard, the tip was grinding against my stomach.

"Go wash your face, and come right back," I told her.

Once I heard the bathroom door close, I took off my T-shirt and flopped down onto the bed. I pulled the blanket back, got my feet under it, and tucked the rest of it over me, my head sinking into the pillow.

My contract with Shawn was for three years. I couldn't have him find out what happened in this room, and I couldn't have him pissed off at me. I was just starting my career. This wasn't a good way to kick it off.

But, damn, that girl was seductive as fuck.

And I wanted her.

And I'd have her the second she returned to this bed.

I'd taste. I'd eat. I'd kiss every inch of that skin until she was screaming so loud, the only thing left to give her was my cock.

As I waited for her, I thought about how her pussy would feel.

How warm it would be.

How tight it would clench my dick.

And, just as I imagined what she would look like naked, I heard the sound of the bathroom door. My eyes shot to the entryway as I waited for her to step out. It took her a few seconds to round the corner. When she did, I saw that she'd taken her jeans off, and she was standing in front of me in just her strapless bra and a pair of matching panties.

"Get over here," I ordered.

She stopped when she reached the foot of the bed. "What are you going to do to me, handsome?"

"I'm going to fucking devour you."

She shook her head, a smile growing over that gorgeous face. "You're a naughty man, Jack Hunt."

"Naughty doesn't happen until I rip off those panties and put my tongue on your pussy."

———————

With my head pounding from how much I'd drunk last night, I gently opened my eyes and slid out from underneath Samantha's arms, getting up to search for my ringing phone. I found it in my jacket and turned off the alarm I'd set.

It was a little past six, which meant my flight was in three hours.

Knowing I needed food more than a shower, I put my feet through the leg holes of my boxer briefs. Once those were on, my pants were next, followed by all the other clothes I'd dropped on the floor last night.

I went into the bathroom to do a quick brush of my teeth before tossing all my shit into my suitcase, which I rolled to the door.

Samantha hadn't moved in the bed. Her hair was fanned across the white pillow, the blanket pulled up to her neck. I leaned down and pressed my lips against her forehead.

"Good-bye, gorgeous girl," I whispered into her cheek.

She didn't even stir.

I went to the door, taking one last look behind me, and then I closed it, moving down the long hallway.

After a long cab ride, I checked in at the airport, and once I reached my gate, I reclined in one of the seats and took out my phone. It was late in LA, but I had a feeling Brett would still be up.

Me: Yo, you awake?
Brett: How was last night?

Me: *The draft was sick. Fifth? That's some serious shit. I still can't believe it.*

Brett: *You worked hard for that one. Cha-ching.*

Me: *And I partied hard to celebrate. I'm hungover as fuck.*

Brett: *Are you going to make your flight?*

Me: *Yeah, I'm good. So, I met the girl of my fucking dreams.*

Brett: *And?*

Me: *Best sex I've ever had in my life.*

Brett: *Then, why don't you bump your flight a couple of days and spend some more time with her?*

Me: *I can't have her.*

Brett: *Why?*

Me: *She's Shawn Cole's little sister.*

Brett: *Fuck, man, you're right. Cut that shit off right now. Don't risk it. It's career-ending; you know that. Remember, clients first. Always.*

Me: *Mother. Fucker. I'll see you when I get home.*

If you would like to keep reading, click HERE *to purchase Endorsed.*